CONVERGENCE
BOOK ZERO

MASS DESTRUCTION

G.W. MULLINS

LIGHT OF THE MOON PUBLISHING

ISBN: 978-1-958221-08-2

First Printing

Light Of The Moon Publishing has allowed this work to remain exactly as the author intended, verbatim, without editorial input.

Printed in the United States of America

For further information, on his writing, visit G.W. Mullins' web site at http://gwmullins.wix.com/books

For books available from G.W. Mullins in Hardback, Paperback and eBook

Visit: https://gwmullins.wixsite.com/books

Or scan the QR Code below

What begins as a simple, bittersweet tale about a man turned into a polar bear, grandly unfolds into a rich, mythical adventure, in this best-selling book series.

Based on Hans Christian Andersen's fairy tale, author G.W. Mullins expands on this classic story creating a new mythology that takes readers into the land of snow and ice.

G.W. Mullins

Rise Of The Snow Queen
Book Series

The Polar Bear King

War Of The Witches

The Story of Gerda and Kai

Rise Of The Snow Queen Series

What begins as a simple, bittersweet tale about a man turned into a polar bear, grandly unfolds into a rich, mythical adventure in this best-selling book series.

Based on Hans Christian Andersen's fairy tale, author G.W. Mullins expands on this story creating a new mythology that takes readers into the world of snow and ice.

Long before the adventures of Gerda and Kai, this story takes readers to a remote mountain village, where winter claims lives, at the Snow Queen's command. The story goes back to the Mirror and how it cracked, sending its shards into the world to infect the innocent.

This reimagining, embarks on a much more adult tone with the mood turning rather sinister, as the Snow Queen battles to obtain the mirror. The story will capture and pull you in as Gerda and Kai make their appearances by the third book in the series.

Rise Of The Snow Queen Series

Book One: The Polar Bear King

Book Two: The War Of The Witches

Book Three: The Story Of Gerda And Kai

From
The
Dead
Of
Night
Book Series
Death is only the beginning.
Daniel walked in the land of the Dead.
Now the Dead want him back
Daniel Is Waiting
Daniel Returns
Daniel Awakens
Daniel's Fate
GW Mullins

From the Dead Of Night Series

Death Is Only The Beginning. Daniel walked in the land of the dead. Now the dead want him back!

Daniel Stratton died in a tragic accident. His life should have been over, but it was not. His spirit spent the next sixty years trying to communicate with the people who came to the cemetery. Then, Jen came one night to the mausoleum, seeking refuge from a life that was spinning out of control. It was there she found Daniel.

As they work to free him from the cemetery; they learn that the Light comes for all dead, Daniel is forced to enter it. Inside he sees seven Shadow People within the light, and each one marks him. Daniel knows these Shadows will come for him. Each one in the body of human who has just died. To survive, Daniel and Jen must escape the "Shadows" that are coming for them.

From the Dead Of Night Series

Book One: Daniel Is Waiting

Book Two: Daniel Returns

Book Three Daniel Awakens

Book Four: Daniel's Fate

Best-Selling Author G.W. Mullins speaks to the
dead and talks about
After Death Communication in his book series...

Messages
From The
Other Side

Stories of the Dead, Their Communication, and Unfinished Business

Messages From The Other Side

Crossing Over

Available in Hardback, Paperback and eBook

Messages From The Other Side Series

Best-selling author G.W. Mullins shares his personal journey towards understanding death, the afterlife and communication with spirits of loved ones who have passed over. In "Messages From The Other Side Stories of the Dead, Their Communication, and Unfinished Business," Mullins tells of dealing with the grief of his mother passing and the reassurance of an after death communication that totally changed his outlook towards death and grief.

This book not only tells of Mullins' personal journey into understanding but also guides others to understand why we receive communications and the signs to look for. Mullins also explores visitation dreams and tells of his own personal experience in the area and shares the stories of others who have had similar experiences.

This book highlights the author's personal journey in an exploration for knowledge, and his understanding, without question, there is life after death.

Messages From The Other Side Series

Book One: Meassages From The Other Side

Book Two: Crossing Over

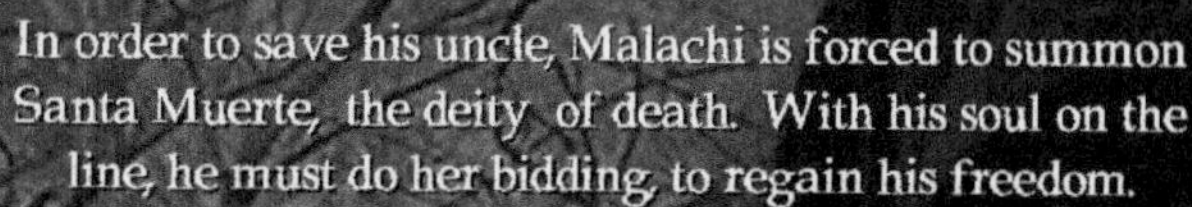

Rise Of The Dark Lighter Series

Mullins returns to the familiar world he created for the "From The Dead Of Night" series, while building a new story in this universe. In the book "Daniel's Fate," Mullins left his audience with an ending that promised more. In this latest book, he delivers with a continuation of the final battle between good and evil.

In order to save his uncle, Malachi is forced to summon Santa Muerte, the deity of death. He offers a year of his life in exchange for her help. With his soul on the line, he must do her bidding, to regain his freedom.

The dead begin to rise, as Angels and Demons prepare to wage war for control of humanity. Malachi must choose a side as Armageddon begins.

"Dark Awakening" is the first of three books from "Rise Of The Dark Lighter." This new series is a continuation of his "From The Dead Of Night" books.

Rise Of The DarkLighter

Book One: Dark Awakening

Book Two: Night Of The Demon

Danni liked the quiet upstate New York house she had moved to...
Until she realized something else was living in the house with her.

VENGEANCE

G.W. MULLINS

SOMETIMES
THE THINGS YOU CANNOT SEE,
CAN BE THE MOST DEADLY.

G.W.
Mullins

Available worldwide in Hardback, Paperback and eBook

Vengeance
A Paranormal Murder Mystery

*"Mystery, Murder, Paranormal Events, and a story
that leaves you guessing as the bodies stack up."
– Matthew Trent OutLoud Magazine*

After the death of her father, Danni starts a new life
in a seaside town in New York where she and her
mother move into a strange Gothic house with a
terrible history. From the moment Danni gets there,
she feels she is being watched. She is sure they are
not alone in the house.

As Danni learns of her new home, she is told of a
past resident who fell to her death on the nearby cliffs
at the same time that her teenaged daughter,
Elizabeth, disappeared.

Elizabeth's spirit, appears to Danni and claims that
her mother's death was a murder, not suicide and asks
for Danni's help in bringing the dangerous killer to
justice.

The mystery unfolds as Danni enlists the help of the
hunky new friend she has made named Joe. A
romance develops between them, but does Joe know
more about the murder and disappearance than he is
letting on? Will Danni live to solve the murder?

As the city darkens and humans descend into sleep, a powerful entity known as the Sand Man, takes control of our dreams and nightmares.

DREAM WALKER

Don't Fall Asleep,
The SandMan Is Coming!

Enter The SandMan

Wide Awake In Dreamland

Available in Hardback, Paperback and eBook

G.W. Mullins

Dream Walker Series

They say a dream is a wish, but what they forgot to mention, nightmares are dreams too. As the city darkens and humans descend into sleep, a powerful being enters the Earth Realm. This mysterious creature, known as the Sandman, takes control of our dreams and battles for control of souls.

After a boy named Zach is taken into the other realm, he awakens to a new world filled with nightmares. He is joined by two others, Daniel and Jen, as they battle to escape the Dream World, and find their way back to reality. Beware the Sandman is coming.

"Enter The Sandman" is the first of three books from Author G.W. Mullins' "Dream Walker" book series. This new series, shares a couple of familiar faces from the Best-Selling "From The Dead Of Night" books, featuring the Best-Selling titles "Daniel Is Waiting" and "Daniel Returns."

Dream Walker Series

Book One: Enter The SandMan

Book Two: Wide Awake In Dreamland

Nick Grainger
Book One
The Curse Of Cleopatra
G.W. Mullins

Nick Grainger Series

Building on the concept that the Earth was once populated by a superior Ancient Alien race, this new book series takes the reader on an adventure through gateways to the multiverse.

Nick Grainger, a young college student working on an archaeological dig in Egypt, accidentally activates a gate to a different universe. He along with three of his companions, are thrown into the ancient alien gateway system between parallel worlds. Lost in the multiverse, they must search for a way home.

On their journey, their gate opens into strange new worlds, similar to their Earth, but in different times and in places. It is on one such Earth, they arrive in Egypt, not as it was in the days of the ancients. Now, it is a place where a technologically advanced race of gods rule.

These new gods of Egypt live through taking the bodies of human hosts. It is there, Nick must fight his ultimate battle, as he is designated to be host to the god Anubis.

"Nick Grainger The Curse Of Cleopatra" is the first of three books from Author G.W. Mullins' "Nick Grainger" book series.

FROM THE AUTHOR OF "RISE OF THE SNOW QUEEN - THE POLAR BEAR KING" AND "DANIEL IS WAITING"
THE LEGEND OF
WHITE BEAR
EVERYONE HAS A
BEAST WITHIN THEM.
G.W.
MULLINS
FROM THE AUTHOR OF "RISE OF THE SNOW QUEEN - THE POLAR BEAR KING" AND "DANIEL IS WAITING"

The Legend Of White Bear

In this Native American influenced novel, Mullins pulls on his own Native American heritage and mixes it with shapeshifting fantasy. The outcome, is a story that pulls you in, and keeps you guessing until the end.

Native American tribes had many stories of the bear. Many also believed in shapeshifters, where tribesmen could become animals. One of these stories is of a Cherokee girl named Nita.

Her tribe faced the bear every full moon. When the bear came, many would die. To protect his daughter, the chief sent her away to live in a rip in time and space, called the void. He told her it was for her protection, but he never told her of the bear history.

One member of his tribe, was burdened with carrying the bear trait. For a lifetime, they would be cursed with being both human and bear until their death. Then a new child would be born to carry the trait. While in the void, Nita discovers the history of the white bear, and her people's inheritance.

Other titles available from G.W. Mullins include:

Timeless - An Adult Paranormal Romance Novel

Aliens, Gods, And Other Paranormal Native American Tales

The Native American Story Book Volume 1-5- Stories Of The American Indians For Children

Walking With Spirits Volumes 1-6 Native American Myths, Legends, And Folklore

The Native American Cookbook

Star People, Sky Gods And Other Tales of The Native American Indians

More Star People, Sky Gods and Other Paranormal Tales Of The Native American Indians

For Clarence

"I know not with what weapons World War III will be fought, but World War IV will be fought with sticks and stones."

Albert Einstein

"If we don't end war, war will end us."

H. G. Wells

THE
CONVERGENCE
BEGINS

Chapter 0 - The End Is Now

"Why do you look so scared, Comrade Patrick?" The Russian cosmonaut asked, as he laughed studying the other man's reflection in the glass of his console.

"I'm not scared, so much as, I don't know how to react to the experience of floating free in space. I mean, this is the real thing." He replied.

"You chose to accept the position of captain of this space ship they are building. What do they call it now? Discovery?"

"Who knows what it is called this week. All I know is, they are putting me through every training that is known to man." Patrick said, shaking his head as he turned to look out of the space station's window.

"I would not worry, if they chose you, then they must be sure of your abilities. Besides, you may end up being one of the few who survive. Tensions are great, war is eminent. If your ship gets off the ground, you and the people living on it, may be the last people of Earth."

"Wow, thanks…that was not too much pressure to put on me."

"Calm yourself, the space walk will commence in 15 minutes. You had better get suited up."

"Pavel, can I ask you something?" Patrick said staring into the man's face.

"Yes, what would you like to know?"

"If World War 3 does break out, would we still be friends?"

The Russian began to laugh, "What makes you think we are friends now? I am only kidding. We have known each other for some time. I do not trust very many people. You, I trust with my life. We would probably be friends no matter what."

Patrick turned and floated down the corridor. His stomach turned at the thought of what was before him. He doubted himself, and the role he would lead in saving mankind. If the war did not kill humanity, the state of the environment was about to.

The environmental crisis that was spreading across the earth was unrepairable. The planet would be uninhabitable in less than five years. The governments knew it was coming for decades, yet they did nothing until it was too late. Now, instead of doing whatever they could to save lives, they were on the verge of nuclear war.

A group of scientists came together and formed the concept of the ship Discovery. It would serve as a record of human life, and a way to preserve a small group of humans. The ship would feature the latest in space pod living, and feature holographic technology, that would create a world that looked just as the earth did, for the regions the groups of people would be taken from. In a sense, they would never know they had been relocated to the ship. There could be no mass hysteria, if the people were unaware, they even left their homes.

The real challenge was, to get Patrick trained and the ship completed before the first nuke was launched. The estimated departure was to come in two weeks. There was no time for error, or unsureness of the new ship's captain. Patrick knew this, as he began to pull on his space suit. Breathing deeply, he was no amateur and he knew it. Lives depended on him.

As the door opened into deep space, Patrick stared out in awe. It was everything he had hoped it to be. His fears were behind him, as a smile crossed his face. He checked his readings one last time as he floated in the doorway.

"Well, are you going to float there all day, or are you going out?" Pavel teased him.

"I am going out. Oh, and Pavel, don't let anything happen while I am out there." Patrick joked.

"What could happen? There is nothing going on here except space. Maybe the settlement on the moon's surface might drift past as you are finally going out the door."

"I cannot believe we finally settled the moon." Patrick said looking towards the lights on the surface. "Man, that is beautiful."

As Patrick finished his last words, he floated outwards away from the station's doorway. He breathed deeply, as he moved around and saw the earth below him. He didn't know what to think, being so far away looking in. He finally found his strength and courage.

Patrick turned around and looked back to the moon. The structures were very clear to him from his distance. They looked like a small city, like you would find in some quiet corners of the earth. Except, there were no quiet corners anymore. The days of quiet were gone years ago. They went with the plague that came after Covid. Too many lives were lost, too many mistakes were made. No one knew of the side effects the cure would have.

As Patrick floated deep in his thoughts, a bright light shot in his direction. He struggled to see what was going on. "Pavel, what was that?" He waited, but there was nothing except silence. Then a second blast, and he knew what was happening.

As the moon rattled, and then debris shot into space, a huge chunk of rock flew at Patrick. He pulled at his harness feverishly, quickly moving out of the way. Then as his body drifted in space, he turned and saw the destruction. The moon was blasted in two, separated almost down the center. The lights on the surface came from nuclear explosions. He was sure of that. "Pavel, do you hear me?"

"Yes, Comrade, it was nuclear in nature. Word is spreading across all channels. There have been explosions back home as well. You are ordered to come back to the station. We are at war. It has begun…the end of life as we know it is upon us."

Chapter 1 – Six Months Ago

"Hostilities are growing between the United States and Russia. While the United Nations is struggling to bring some resolution, several other countries have entered the hostilities, many of which are communist. The fear of war is looming."

The sound from the monitor speakers echoed throughout the former NASA space center. The massive work force stopped in unison, as they looked towards the screens which lined the massive halls. In that moment, there was no other sound, but the news anchor's voice.

Many bowed their heads in silent prayer, for a solution to the inevitable event that was coming fast upon them. Others turned back to their work. They knew if they did not finish as scheduled, there would be no reason to build the massive metal structure, that rested between the buildings in front of them.

Patrick walked the hall, making his way to the command center. As he looked out of the window, onto the puzzle pieces before him, he could see the ship taking shape. He shook his head, thinking this ship was like something out of an old space movie. If it worked, it would be spectacular.

The ship was broken into several pod cities, which sat side by side on the outer platform. All of which would be connected by a main central ship. The ship even had its own agricultural pod, to constantly produce food and oxygen. Patrick smiled, as he realized he would captain this massive star ship.

His joy turned, as Patrick faced the reality, that only a select group of people would be chosen to go into space. He found it cruel that the whole process of saving human kind would be cloaked in deceit. Those left behind, would certainly die as the global ecosystem disintegrated, from pollution or radiation.

He felt a lump in his throat, as he faced the reality, that family and friends would not survive. Today, that would not be his greatest concern. Discovery had to be finished on time. So far, that seemed like an attainable goal.

"It's beautiful, isn't it?" A female voice came from behind him.

"Yes, it is. I just never thought it would come to this." He answered.

"I am Major Carter. I am supervising the pods construction and testing all holographic installations into the cities within."

"Hello, I am Alexander Patrick. I am for lack of a better term, the captain."

"I am aware. Don't let it overwhelm you. This is a great honor to be chosen to head this ship. You are going to save a lot of lives."

"Yeah, and they won't even know it. They will go to bed one night, and then wake up the next morning, not even knowing they are on a space ship transplanted into a holographic world, not of their choosing." Patrick grumbled.

"It is necessary. If word got out that we were selecting individuals to go on this ship, or even that the ship existed, we would be bombarded with people trying to force their way onboard. We can barely handle the size of the group we are taking. There just is no fair way to go about this." She sighed knowing she was never going to make herself believe it, let alone another person.

"Will we really make the deadline?" He asked.

"Yes, I believe we will, as long as no one sets off a nuke. Seems like many countries have their fingers ready to push the launch buttons."

"Carter, you are very high up in the government. So, you would know…what are the chances of anyone surviving if multiple warheads are launched?"

"Life on earth as we know it, would be gone. There are safer locations and chances some people would find safety, but radiation would wash over the planet. Whatever would still exist, would be changed, and civilization would crumble. All major cities would soon be uninhabitable. Ever watch a zombie movie?"

Patrick turned back to the window and swallowed hard. He knew she was right. Then, he felt guilty, he was going to survive the possible holocaust, while millions died. He thought hard, and then forced the unsettled feeling to the bottom of his stomach. He had to be strong. People would be depending on him.

He turned back, and looked at Carter. "What about you?"

"What about me?" She asked

"What will happen to you?"

"I will be going with you. I have been granted passage on the ship. You will need someone to head engineering, and I am as qualified as anyone." She said smiling.

"Good, I am happy you will be safe."

"None of us will be safe, until this ship breaks free from the atmosphere, and gets out of attack range."

"You think they would shoot us down? That is crazy." He said in anger.

"No, that is real life, and in a war, you take down the one with the advantage. They don't want to see us succeed, while they stay behind to die. In a rational world, I would like to think everyone would like us to make it into space. Then…there is nothing ration about nuclear war."

"I guess, we work to make this happen. No matter how we have to do it."

"I hear they have a series of training sessions for you. Including a spacewalk. I can only imagine what that will be like."

Patrick looked upwards, staring into the sky. He had never been outside the earth's atmosphere.

He craved the experience, still he had an element of fear inside him. He wondered if it was all too much too soon.

Carter walked over and placed her hand on his shoulder. He turned to her and smiled. He knew she was trying to comfort him, but he had his own demons to deal with. She smiled back at him as they both turned to the window and looked upwards. Their future was right in front of them.

Mullins

Chapter 2 – The Ship of The Future

The morning news, brought the world one step closer to the brink. North Korea, once again went against threats from the world, and tested another nuclear warhead.   The explosion came with a warning to the United States. Any interference would result in retaliation.

President Jones, stood his ground, as he defended the country and his pride. Even he knew, there was no winning in this war. We were doomed, no matter who fired first. He could only hope to hold out until Discovery was launched.

The weeks flew past, as Patrick saw his spacewalk approaching. The ship began to take shape, as the massive dome cities were attached to the main body. In the days after, Patrick walked the ship, and took in all he would be captain of.   He had grown up watching Star Trek, and he tried to think of this as his enterprise. It was a far cry from being that advanced, but it was so much more than he expected.

As he entered the first dome city, the hologram, automatically engaged. An electric grid formed all around him, and as he watched, the shapes of metal walls and glass windows disappeared. Where there were once smooth metallic shapes, there were now glowing lines which converged together taking form.

On the massive floor before him, the shapes of buildings and grassy fields took emerged. Patrick stood back in awe of the holograms. He had never seen anything like it before. In a matter of seconds, a small country town was erected.

Patrick walked in the field of grass, that swayed in the breeze. He kneeled down, and ran his hand through the blades. It felt real. He knew in his mind it was a projected material, but to his sense of touch, it was still real.

He fell back onto the ground. Laughing out loud, he could not contain himself. It was all real to him, from the plants, to the sound of birds in the trees. Even the feeling as the breeze caressed his cheek. He couldn't tell the difference.

Then, he thought of those who would be transplanted there. They would not know either. They would just think, they were home. It was still a lie, but they would know no difference. At least he thought, they would still be alive.

"I see you have come to know Carson Corners."

Patrick flipped around to see Carter heading his way. "Yes, this is so much more than I expected. It feels like I am on earth. I did not know things like this were possible."

"It wasn't, until very recently, and then we kept it a secret, since it has so many military applications."

"Something so wonderful, that could be used for so many good things, has to be hidden from those who would abuse it." Patrick reached out and touched the grass, trying to understand why people abused so much in the world.

"Welcome to the real world." Carter said walking away.

"Well, almost. The world we soon would have lived in."

"This one has its advantages. Like health care, and controlled weather. You can even summon help, if you know what to ask for. Watch this…emergency care needed, medical."

As she finished speaking, directly in front of them, a distortion in the holographic field formed. The image of a man took shape, as a brilliant light swirled in place.

"I am Holo-tech Medical Assistant 1, please state your emergency." The figure stood before them, as the light he emitted flicked and fizzled.

"Hmm, that is strange, he is having trouble taking form. I'll have to look into that, it should not be happening. Still, it is new, and there is always some issue to fix." Carter said staring at the hologram.

"PPPPPlease state your emergency." The hologram asked.

"There is no emergency. This is only a test. One that is failing miserably. Disengage Medical Assistant. This will have to be looked into"

As Carter spoke, the hologram disappeared into the electrical grid. Patrick watched in disbelief of the technology, as everything returned to normal. The hologram system was intelligent, and could add to itself at will.

"Carter, if the people living here are not supposed to know about the hologram, how are you going to use the medical assistant?"

"Easy, he will appear, as if in a hospital setting or as a doctor making a house call. He can change himself to fit any situation, just like the holographic grid can adapt to fit the need. We can add terrain, add buildings, or add road and land as a person travels. In most cases the hologram moves, the person does not."

"This will take some getting used to. All I ever saw a hologram do was perform in concert." Patrick said knowing he was out of his ballpark.

"Oh, you saw those disgusting holographic pop stars? They were awful, I am glad they have been phased out. Still, if we didn't start there, we would not have gotten to this point. Now, imagine a complete town or city like this in each pod, fully functional, programmed to expand and create new things as needed."

"I would say that is a lot of room for error." He laughed.

"Unfortunately, and that is why we are testing and perfecting before Discovery gets off the ground. In space, is nowhere to find out, we made a mistake."

"At least, you will be there to help fix what may go wrong."

"I would rather get it right before liftoff."

As the two walked forward, the land before them, extended and continued in any direction they chose to go. The hologram seemed to work in every way, except where creating people was concerned. That seemed like the least of their problems.

Chapter 3 – Artificial Intelligence

The stars seemed to glow a little brighter, as Patrick walked down the long corridor of the Discovery. He tried to hide his smile from those who passed. He was proud of his title of Captain, but also scared. A fear gripped him deep inside, one that awakened his lack of confidence. He tried not to let others see his inner saboteur.

At the end of the corridor, he entered the lift, and headed for the bridge of the ship. The doors closed, as an automated voice asked where he would like to go. He looked at the diagram of the ship, and stalled for a moment. He was unaccustomed to the systems that surrounded him. In a low muted voice, he said, "To the bridge."

The system acknowledged him, as it slowly started to move. Patrick stared at the computer screen, as he noticed he was barely moving. Before he could open his mouth, and question the lift's slowness, it lurched forward and then slammed him sideways.

Patrick flew to the floor, slamming his head in the process. A slight trickle of blood, made its way down his forehead. He sat up and tried to gain his balance, as the lift surged again.

Grabbing onto the hand railing, Patrick pulled himself to the emergency shutoff. The lift surged one final time, as he held on in fear of what might happen next. As the doors to the lift opened, Patrick was thrown outwards, and onto the carpeted floor of the bridge.

He lifted his head, as the stream of blood made its way down his cheek. Before him, stood the full complement of the bridge crew. An ensign shouted "Captain on the bridge," just before Patrick rested on his knees.

"Are you OK sir?" the second in command approached him.

"Yeah, I just don't think the lift likes me very much. Does that happen often?" Patrick asked.

"I am sorry sir; we are working on getting the bugs out. It just seems…there are a lot of bugs. Oh, I apologize, I am Stephens, your second in command."

"Nice to meet you. You wouldn't happen to have a bandage, would you?"

"I am so sorry sir; I will help you with that. Emergency medical hologram assistance needed." He called out.

"PPPPlease state your emergency." The electronic voice rang out.

"Wow, that's not right." Stephens said, as he staired at the hologram. "He is supposed to be solid mass, and what is with the glitches."

"I saw the same thing in the pod for Carson Corners. I think we have a bit of a problem. Is there no human doctor onboard?" Patrick said, as he raised a hand to his head, to try to stop the bleeding.

"No sir, there is no human doctor. We were told the holograms would be able to do it all." Stephens' voice trailed off, as he approached the hologram, and tried to touch his finger to it.

"Do you mind? I am not accustomed to humans trying to disturb my energy force." The hologram snapped back.

"Wait, did the medical hologram, just cop and attitude? This is wrong, very wrong." Patrick said, turning to Stephens. "Get this thing fixed, or take it offline. It is of no use to us like this."

"Yes sir, I will."

"Oh, and Stephens."

"Yes, sir?"

"Please, stop calling me sir. We can be a little more relaxed, it's not like we have launched." Patrick spoke, as an ensign approached him with a cloth, and attempted to clean the smeared blood from his face.

Stephens went about addressing the issue of the malfunctioning hologram. He studied the diagnostics in the computer, and then ran a full check of the ships systems. Standing in the background, the hologram watched all that went on around him. As Stephens studied the hologram, it studied the ship and its systems. This, was more than any mere hologram, it was artificial intelligence beyond its original design.

"Captain, do you want the good news or the bad news?" Stephens asked.

"Preferably, good news would be better, being the state of the ship and the world for that matter are in play here." Patrick tried to be humorous.

"I can't shut him down."

"What the hell do you mean, you can't shut him down? He is a hologram, just turn his system off."

"I tried; it is as if it has control of itself. I shut down the system, and it reboots itself."

"Can someone be controlling this 'hologram' from the outside?"

"No, we have a dampening field all around the ship, for security, so no one can find out about it. This is from inside, there is an intelligence here."

"Could that be why so many things are malfunctioning?

Patrick said, as he walked circles around the medical hologram.

"I would say yes captain. We have to control this, and correct the problem, before we launch into space. We cannot afford to leave orbit, to find out we have lost control of the ship." Stephens could not hide the look of concern that covered his face.

"How do we get it out of the system?"

"We could shut everything down, and purge the program."

"Or, you could let me do my job, and correct the problem." Carter added as she stepped out of the lift.

"I was wondering when you would get here." Patrick said grinning at her.

"Well, I am here, and no, you will not purge my systems from the ship. We can isolate the sub-commands of the hologram system, eliminate the conflict and cleanse the medical hologram without damaging years of my work."

"Then please, have at it. The floor is yours Carter, take care of our not so little problem."

"I promise you; it will not be so easy to eradicate me from the system." The hologram spoke up.

Carter turned to the hologram, and looked on in fear. She had no idea how it had taken control.

Chapter 4 – The Last Christmas

The hologram stared at them intently, studying their actions, and anticipating their next move. Deep inside its programming, it was contemplating how to survive the situation. Being a machine, it had no human emotions, but its desire to live was strong.

It watched Carter, as she scanned the computer files, looking for the way someone had broken in, and implanted the program. She scanned line after line of programming and then she found it.

Someone had implanted the programming, long before the ship was brought online. One of the crew was responsible. There was an outside agent onboard, posing as one of the crew. She could not believe it possible. She had worked so closely with all these people, yet one of them got past her.

"Captain, may I see you in your office privately?"

"Yes, you may." Patrick answered, and thanked the crewman who bandaged him.

She led Patrick to the private office, just to the rear of the bridge. Closing the door behind, she scanned the area for listening devices. She looked at Patrick, with a stern look on her face.

"That hologram is not one of mine."

"What do you mean? If it is not yours, then whose is it?"

"One of the crew implanted it." She responded.

"OK, why?"

"To sabotage this flight and wreck our chances of getting into space. Or even worse, copy this ship and help some other country build their own, with our technology. "

"Damn…if that is so, then they know what we are doing. We will have to move faster, if we are going to get off the ground before they try to shut us down." Patrick was furious. How could this have happened? "Then we have no other choice. You have to wipe the infected systems. Can you replace the corrupted hologram with your own original programming?"

"Yes, I have the backed-up files. It may not be so hard to do, but what if there are any other A.I. files onboard, working in the background?"

"I guess we deal with it when the time comes. But for now, get that out-of-control saboteur off my ship. Oh, and how about we start looking for who might have installed that hologram in the first place."

Carter returned to the control panel, and isolated the program from the rest of the ship. She watched as the hologram studied her. It was in survival mode, and was prepared to stop her progress. As Carter prepared to delete the program, the hologram stared at the console, and fed energy to it, until it built a charge in the metal surrounding the unit. As Carter reached out, to push the final button to delete the hologram, a bolt of energy shot out and entered her body.

She jerked back and forth as the hologram exacted its revenge, and electrocuted her. Patrick saw the surge hit, as he scanned for anything he could use, to separate her from the charge. Just behind the control deck was a huge rubber pipe shielding. He grabbed it, wedged it between Carter and the controls, knocking her backwards.

As she flew across the room, the energy that almost killed her was disbursed. Patrick saw his opportunity, and lunged at the keyboard, finishing the task. As the process initiated, the hologram jerked violently, as if it were torn apart from the inside out. Then in a final movement, it disappeared from sight.

Carter sat up, with the aid of one of the crew members, "Is that thing gone?"

"Yes, I just finished what you started."

"Too bad, I wanted to kick that thing's ass. It tried to electrocute me."

"Well, it is over now. It is gone, now run a full ship wide diagnostic. I want to make sure there are no more infected systems." Patrick insisted.

"I'm on it." Carter insisted.

"No, I am sure Stephens is more than capable. You almost died; I think you need some fresh air for a little while."

Carter said nothing, as she saw Patrick was right. They walked towards the lift and prepared to enter. Patrick shook his head, as he took her arm and led her to the stairwell. She laughed at him, as she realized the humor in it all.

As the door closed, Stephens took to the console and scanned the ship. He looked on intently as the ship's systems passed in front of his eyes. One after one came up clean, and then he found the backup bridge system, which was hidden from the rest of the crew. He smiled as he studied the programming. It was safe. No one knew of it but him. His creation was still alive. No one would find it until they were deep in space, where it would be too late.

As Patrick and Carter left the ship, they looked out across the protected space center to a private corner, where a tree was decorated and lights had been strung all around the scaffolding. Patrick staired on at the beauty of it, and realized with all that had happened and was about to, it was nearing Christmas. He had almost forgotten.

"You know, this will be our last Christmas on earth." He said softly under his voice."

"I guess you are right. I had been so wrapped up in getting the ship completed, I lost all track of time."

"Do you think, if anyone survives, that they will miss us." He asked her.

"Maybe. I guess the big question is, will anyone survive?" She said taking a deep breath.

"Who would have thought it would come to this. We finally pushed everything to the edge of destruction. Now, all someone has to do is hit the final button.”

"So, what does it feel like to be one of the last survivors of earth?” She laughed.

"We haven’t gotten off the ground yet. I will answer that question, when we break free of the atmosphere. Until then, I am just going to stand here, enjoy the twinkling lights, and soak in the last Christmas. Merry Christmas Carter.”

"Same to you Patrick. And hopefully, many more.”

Chapter 5 – Nuclear Winter

Patrick walked alone across the frozen landscape. He felt a snowflake land on his cheek, as he turned to look at the Discovery. He thought to himself, if they could pull this off, mankind might just survive in one form or another. As he looked off into the distance, the reality sat in. In a short time, the planet might be a distant memory.

Many things raced through his mind, the memories of family and friends were weighing heavily on him. For a moment, he let the sadness take him, before realizing he had a job to do. If he did not get his ship ready and save the people he could, it would not matter. They all would be doomed.

Patrick turned to reenter the building, and head for the cafeteria. He couldn't remember the last time he had eaten. It didn't seem as important at the time, but he had to keep his strength up. As he rounded the end of the hall, the smell of food slapped him in the face, with a force he could not stop.

The food smelled bad, and not just a light smell you could ignore. This smell, was more of an overpowering skunk, that had been dead on the road for a few days. He drew back and wondered if it was worth the experience to enter the doorway. He knew he had to keep his strength up, he had to find something he could stomach.

As he walked through the room, he smiled as he thought, this might be bad, but what would food grown and created in space be like. Then he reassured himself, it had to be better than this. He continued to the serving line, and looked over the meat that seemed to be coated in a sauce, to make it possibly look like real food.

He looked on, as he tried to not inhale the noxious fumes that arose before him. No, he could not do it. He scanned the wall, looking for any kind of vending machine. There was little to pick from, so he made his way down the line, choosing things that looked like they had been prepackaged. He was no fool, he could not save mankind, if the food killed him first.

As Patrick grabbed his food, he wandered a distance down the hall, until the smell seemed to clear. He found a chair near a window in the hall, and looked out, as the snow picked up. It was beautiful, and he sadly lowered his head, knowing he would not see anything naturally created like this in space.

The quiet place he had found in the hall, was quickly changed with a news alert blasting over the monitor system just above him. "What the hell now?" He said aloud, though no one was near or heard him.

"Russia has issued a threat to the United States of nuclear deployment, if any weapons are supplied to ally forces, in the wake of their assault on Poland. The world had set by and watched the destruction, brought forth by Russia, with the attacks on Ukraine. The president has issued a statement, saying he will not sit idly by, and allow loss of life. This event has brought us one step closer to war. We can only hope for some resolution. If not, this chain reaction will cause serious global destruction. Stay tuned, and we will bring you further information as events unfold." Then, the newsfeed blinked out, and the screen went dead.

Patrick returned his gaze out the window, as the snowflakes softly drifted down to the ground. He shook his head and swallowed his food. There was more going on here than he could make right. He had to stay focused on his appointed job. If all he could do was save a few hundred, then he would count himself lucky.

Finishing his food, Patrick stood and began to make his way down the hallway, as the floor before him began to vibrate. The feeling started out small and then grew. The wave of shock, threw him to his knees, as sirens began to sound around the base. He tried to get back to his feet, by holding a guard rail, and started making his way to the emergency phone just feet away.

"Hello, is anyone there?" He screamed into the phone.

A mechanical voice acknowledged him. "This is a recording. We are experiencing earthquake conditions. Please stay calm and try to make your way to the nearest exit. If you need assistance press 0."

"Great, the place is being ripped apart around me and they want to send me to an operator."

He pushed the button on the phone several times before slamming it with his fist. He screamed out to anyone who could hear, asking what was happening, but no one responded. The sound of the phone changed as a voice rang out.

"What is your emergency?" The female on the line asked.

Patrick held tight to the wall, as the next wave of rumbling started. "Hello, this is Captain Patrick, I am from the Discovery. Please, what is going on out there? Is this an earthquake or more?"

"Captain, what we are experiencing is a regional quake. This whole area is near the center of the disturbance. There is nothing we can do, but sit back and ride it out. Get yourself clear of anything that could collapse on you."

"I thought we scanned this area before the construction started. This should not be happening."

"I know, I hear you. Sadly, this is just another part of the environmental destruction. We cannot predict which areas will disintegrate next. Like they said, we have about five years left until complete destruction. If the nukes don't get us, Mother Nature will. Go be safe until this is done. Good luck Captain Patrick."

Patrick steadied himself in between shock waves, and ran for the nearest exit. Not slowing down, he threw himself into the door release, and fell out to the sidewalk. He felt the pain in his knees, as he impacted onto the cement below. The pain ran through him, as he rolled and propped himself upright.

As he raised his eyes to look to the top of the building, he saw flames, and then an explosion rocked everything around him. He tried to breathe as a single word escaped his lips, "No."

Chapter 6 – Rebuilding A Dream

Patrick held on as the ground rumbled and the explosions continued. He was not a man to let fear rule him, but this situation was pushing his limits. He sat there on the ground for what seemed like an hour, before he rose up, he was tired of the situation. He needed to know how his ship was. In his mind, he was sure it was destroyed.

Running for the side of the building; he dared not try to make his way down the inner building, which looked like it had experienced much damage from the explosions. His legs hurt, as he flew around to the opening, where the ship was being constructed. He stopped dead in his tracks, as he saw the damage.

Parts of the ship were still on fire, from the blasts of the natural gas line, which ran near the construction. He stood frozen, sure in his mind, the ship would never be finished. Sections had fallen and broken, under the weight of the ship shifting and falling from their lifts.

"The crew." He said under his breath, as he began to run to any opening he could find. He clawed his way through a bulkhead the was torn off, and climbed to the inside. It was there he found the first fatality. An engineering officer lay dying at his feet.

Patrick dropped down and took the man's hand. He stared into the man's eyes not knowing what to say. His only words, "I am so sorry this happened."

"This, was not your fault. Hell, I might have been dead in a few months to a year anyway. If the bombs don't get us…who knows if this ship would fly anyway. I guess it is just my time." The man said as he lay on the floor, partially trapped under a large metal wall.

Patrick felt the pain running through him, and the sadness he was experiencing, for he barely knew this man. He would have been one of Discovery's most important crew members. Patrick held tight as the man began to die. This was one lesson they never taught him in all his training. People would die as they launched into space. The ship might fail, and they could all die. This he thought, was the most important lesson to learn.

As the engineer laid there on the floor, Patrick folded the man's arms over his chest. He wished him well on his journey, to wherever he was going. He took a deep breath, as he stood wiping a tear from his eye, before made his way to the bridge.

The going was slow, as all the lifts could not be trusted. He climbed by ladder, floor to floor, until he arrived outside the doors. Pressing the buttons did nothing, they must have been damaged in the explosions. He reached for the manual override and cranked the doors open by hand. He was not ready for what he saw inside.

Crew were strewn all around the floor. He scanned from one crewman to the next, assessing their medical situations. Then he saw her, Carter was sprawled unconscious. He ran to her, calling out her name.

As he kneeled by her side, she opened her eyes. "I think we have a little mess here."

He smiled at her, as he spoke, "It's going to be alright. We will fix it…just might take a minute. Is your medical hologram in place yet?"

"Yes, I reinstalled it just after you left."

"Good, I think we are going to need it. Just hold tight." He said, as he called out for the hologram.

"Please state the purpose of your medical emergency." The hologram spoke as it scanned the room, and its final words trailed off. "Hmm…never mind, I think I understand."

The hologram assessed the many wounded, and split himself into multiple versions, making his way to each individual. He worked quickly to get them all stable, as he used his transporting device, to move them one at a time to the remains of sick bay.

As the final version of the hologram tended to Carter, he concluded she had a slight concussion, and was treatable on the bridge. "Captain, I will go to sick bay now and care for the wounded. If you have further need of me, call."

"Thank you, for your help." Patrick replied.

"That is unusual." The medical hologram replied.

"How's that?" He asked

"Humans are not very appreciative of synthetics or A.I.'s."

"Well, they should be, your roll in this ship is very important and I appreciate any help you give."

"Thank you, Captain. I look forward to working with you." The hologram said as it transported to the sick bay.

"Your attitude seems to have changed a bit." Carter said, as she propped herself up against the railing behind her.

"I guess all it takes, is a reality check to set you in the right direction. Today, was definitely a huge reality check. I thought the ship was destroyed, and I was worried about you, and the crew as well. We need to see how many injuries and deaths have occurred.”

"Deaths?” Carter said, as her expression changed to dread.

"Yes, an engineering officer died. I found him as I entered the ship. We are going to need at least one new crew member.” He said sadly.

"Give me a minute to get back on my feet, and I will begin to take care of all of this.”

"Take your time, you need to heel. We all do, and then we rebuild,” Patrick took to his captain’s seat, and looked around at all the damage. "We will launch on time, one way or another.”

Chapter 7 – Meanwhile on The International Space Station

Pavel Zakharov stared out of the space station window. He had been in space for weeks. His life was now beginning to feel like he was a permanent part of the space station. He longed to return to earth, but he knew that would not be much of an improvement. He feared the possibility of war. He feared death even more.

His placement there was a great honor, but it was not as if he could have decided it for himself. The government had plans for him. He was there as a way to monitor the military capabilities of the other countries. He was no fool, he had been made a spy in a technology race.

It had been only months, since the peoples of several countries, had established colonies on the moon. It was as if, they ran there as if their lives depended on it. Maybe in a way it did. The earth was on a final countdown, and that was a probable reason for the hostilities. Desperate people do desperate things, especially when faced with death.

Pavel was not a desperate man. He was a man who hoped for better, and a life longer than his 36 years. For now, if he reached 40, he counted himself lucky. And then he wondered, what if they destroyed the planet? They would die in the end anyway, but he would be trapped there on the station, waiting to run out of food or oxygen. The thought made him shiver.

As the station swung through space, the moon came into view. Pavel made his way to the window. On the surface, he could see the construction. It looked like little cities or towns. Within them, all their windows were lit. He was sure, he could see Christmas lights among them.

Pavel was not a religious man, but he found the lights comforting. Perhaps, if he was trapped after the destruction, he could make his way to the moon. Then he wondered, if he would be welcome there. With so much hatred in the world, he had no idea. Then he cursed the virus that started it all, and the vaccines, that took away their humanity.

"We deserved better." He said staring out of the window.

A signal sounded throughout the station. The alarming sound, surrounded him echoing through his brain. He knew what it was, an update from Russia. For a moment, he considered not answering, but every move he made had consequences. If he ignored them too long, they could just blast him out of space.

"What is the difference?" he said, turning to face the computer screen.

"Dobriy den comrade. I see you are well." Russian Commander Makarov said slurring his speech, as if he had been drinking too much vodka.

"I am well, despite my concerns for what goes on, back on earth."

"That is none of your concern. You are on the station, doing what is ordered of you. There you will stay, until we have no further use of you. Just remember, you are in good favor right now with your government. If that changed, you would not be an asset. Comprehend?"

"Yes, I understand. For what reason, do I have the pleasure of your communication?"

"Information, Pavel. There is a visitor, who is scheduled to come your way from the United States government. He is to be there to experience outer space onboard a ship and spacewalk."

"And this is important how?" Pavel asked.

"It is important, because we need information from him. It is rumored, that the United States will launch a space ship in the near future, to save many of their citizens. This man, Alexander Patrick, will captain the ship. We want to know all we can about this, and if possible, can we capture it. These American's don't need to take to space."

"And you would take their ship and information, to create your own escape ship of Russian descent?"

"Survival of the fittest Pavel. Better we survive, to continue our people. When he gets there, ask him questions, gain his trust…then get all you can. It will be a shame, when he dies during a spacewalk, yes?"

You want me to kill him? He is innocent."

"None of us are innocent. You yourself know that by experience. Your hands are not clean. Ask your cousin, if you are innocent. I am sure she would say not, especially after what you did to her."

"Why would you say that? You do not know of my life."

"Oh Pavel, we know everything you did since you were a child. That is why we selected you as an agent. You most definitely have the ability to kill. Besides, it is simple…let him get a distance from the station and release his cable. He cannot retaliate from space. He will simply die, when his oxygen runs out. It's not even like you killed him. The vacuum of space, will do all the work for you."

"And, I will have no choice in this matter."

"Oh, but yes, my boy, you do. You can choose to execute his death, or yours. It is that simple. I think you will see the answer very clearly. Kill him. Your country, will reward you for your service…as long as you are agreeable."

"Very well, when will he be here?"

"In four weeks, we will notify you, when he is leaving in route to you. Now, keep your mouth shut Pavel and be a good Comrade.

As the screen went blank, Pavel returned to the window, and stared out at the moon. He wished he was there, with the many settlers. He was not the person his government wanted him to be. He had made mistakes but that was behind him. Now he had to decide, if he was going to be a hired assassin.

Chapter 8 – Under the Same Bright Moon

As the weeks passed, the repairs to the ship continued. Work progressed faster than expected. Everyone knew it was a priority. They were not just saving their own lives, but others would likely die otherwise.

Patrick toured the ship, watching the repairs at times, participating at other times. As he walked, he was reminded that in the past, captains would do a similar walk through, at a time they expected an unwinnable battle. He wasn't sure, if they would have to fight to take off, but he hoped for the safety of all on board, and they would leave with no damage. Still, he felt the foreshadowing of death.

As he made his way through the ship, he found his way to one of the domes, which was yet to come online. He was still in awe, at the wonder of the huge enclosure. He smiled, as he thought of this place as someone's future home. Their chance at life after the destruction.

There, in the center of the dome, he looked up at the moon. He wondered if the colonies there, were safe and what their lives were like. He hadn't seen any images, but was told the settlement was impressive. The thought went through his mind that maybe as the Discovery left earth, they could see the colony, and be seen by them.

As Patrick stood there and looked upwards, he did not realize his surroundings were changing. He turned as he saw something out of the corner of his eye. There was a storm moving in, coming towards the bay, that formed in front of him. He knew this place, it was San Francisco.

He smiled, as he looked at the sloping streets behind him, and Fisherman's Warf in the distance.

He had been there before as a child. He and his parents traveled there to see his aunt and uncle. That was a happy time, he hadn't thought of it in years. It was nice, and then, he thought of his parents. He hadn't seen them in so long. He would have to leave them soon, when the ship launched. He hadn't thought much about it, until now.

"You OK, captain?" the young Ensign Decker asked.

"Are you old enough to be here?"

"I am 20 years old sir. I was top in my class, which I guess helped me along a lot faster."

"You look like you should have been my younger brother." Patrick laughed trying to keep his composure. "I am sorry, I did not mean to offend you."

"No offense taken; I was actually flattered."

"To answer your question, I am fine. Just lost in my thoughts and the future." Patrick replied.

"I've been doing that a lot lately myself. I know I am fortunate to have this opportunity, but I feel kind of guilty for all those who will be left behind. My family wants me to go, but I feel for them." Decker said as he looked upwards to the moon.

"I wonder what will happen to them after we are gone. Maybe they will survive. If they can become independent and produce their own oxygen and food. I hate the idea of abandoning everyone, no matter where they are."

The ensign turned back to him. "If we want to live, then we make the hard choices and carry on. To be honest, I feel safe knowing you are in charge."

"How's that?" Patrick asked.

"From what I see, you are level headed and strong. You care for us as much as yourself. I feel like you would have my back in an emergency. I trust you."

Patrick smiled and reached out his hand to the ensign. "Thanks for the vote of confidence. I needed it, and yes, I do care. We have already lost a few crew members, and not even left the ground. I don't plan to lose anymore."

"Will we be ready on time to launch?"

"We have no choice. The ship has to make it to space before any other disaster happens. We can't afford not to. All we need, is more natural disasters or a foreign government to get wind of us. Don't worry, we have a few weeks left. We will make it."

As Patrick turned to leave the hologram, he had a slight smile cross his face. Maybe convincing someone else, made him feel a little better. There was a confidence in his walk, as he headed to the bridge.

As he entered and took his seat, he studied the crew, that worked in haste to repair each section of the ship. Patrick watched as Carter reviewed the ships computer systems, she had a look on her face. She suspected something was wrong. As she shook her head, she became even more determined. If there was one implanted program, she was sure there could be another.

Chapter 9 – Countdown to Launch

"Captain, there is a personal message coming in for you." The communications officer announced.

"Can you send it to my office?"

"Yes, message transferred."

Patrick headed towards the doors, which opened as he came near. He was still trying to get used to this ship…his ship. He wanted to feel pride in it, but there was little time. He rounded his desk, hit the button below the screen, and accepted the incoming message.

"Captain Patrick, I assume all is going well." The Admiral said, with a concerned look on his face.

"Yes, Admiral Blaylock, as well as could be expected after the recent earthquake. Repairs are almost complete, and I am awaiting new crew members, to replace those who did not survive."

"Yes, about that, we were all sad to hear of the losses. The new officers are being screened now and will complete training in the next two weeks. That should give enough time to get the ship finished, and for you to make it to the space station."

"Yes general, about that. Is this trip into space totally necessary? I am needed here. There is much to be done."

"Look Patrick, we would not be sending you if it were not necessary. You have training there, and hell man, you have never been in space or done a spacewalk. We need you to be at the top of your game, and this is the final stage. Besides, Carter will care for the ship. She is one of the best people we have, and she will not let you, or us down."

"I understand, and I will be ready to go." Patrick conceded,

"Good, because we are moving your time up. We have heard talk of the Russians putting their noses into the space program. Personally, I think they are on to us. If they are, we may be in trouble.

So, we are speeding up the timeline to launch. Tomorrow you will be on a transport towards the International Space Station. Be ready at 10 A.M. for your escort to collect you and make sure you get on the shuttle safely."

"I understand Admiral, may I ask how long we have until launch?" Patrick said, as his knees began to shake.

"We will launch in one week. By New Year's Day, the Discovery will be on its way to deep space, and headed towards a planet that hopefully will act to sustain life, and become your new home."

"And if it doesn't?" Patrick asked.

"Honestly, by the time you find out, we will all probably be dead." The admiral said hanging his head. "You will find a way…you just have to."

"I understand. I'll be ready for tomorrow. Don't expect me to have slept, but I will be ready."

"Patrick, I know this is the biggest task I could ever ask of anyone, but there is a reason it was laid at your doorstep. We all know you will find a way to make this happen."

"To be honest, I am a bit scared. My knees are shaking."

"Oh man, who would not be scared for what you have to do. Just shows you are human. Be proud of that fear, we do not need a cocky, arrogant fool to mess this up. One thing more…when you get there and are celebrating, have a drink for me."

"Will do general. Keep the faith. Patrick out." The screen flickered as the image of the general faded away.

Patrick sat there at his desk, looking at the screen. He was torn about the timeline being sped up. He thought of his parents. He wanted to tell them everything, but knew he could not. He wanted to hear their voices again.

As he reached for the contacts list on his computer, he wondered what it would solve to talk to them again. Perhaps them not knowing was better. Most of the people worldwide were ignorant to the coming disaster. They were too distracted with the threat of war, to see the environmental collapse.

The screen lit up as Patrick's mother's face appeared before him. He tried to smile and hide his real feelings. His mother's face changed immediately when she saw him. She was proud of her son and missed him. She had no idea of his future, just concern for his health.

"Alexander, I did not expect you. Is something wrong love?" She asked.

"No mom, does something have to be wrong for me to call you?" He laughed.

"Well, as infrequently as I hear from you, maybe I worry more. It wouldn't hurt you to call more often."

"Yeah, I know, where's dad?"

"He is at a doctor's appointment. He will be upset he missed you."

"Is he sick?"

"Who knows, who can tell the difference between sickness and old age these days. He has never been right since the pandemic. Then the vaccine messed with is respiratory system. You know your father; it will take the earth exploding to kill him off."

"Yeah, I guess so. Look mom, I am going on a mission, and I might be away for a while. So, I just wanted to let you know not to worry." He heard his voice change; he was reverting to sounding like a kid again, talking to his mother.

"I can't ask where you are going or what you are doing. Right?" She asked sarcastically.

"That is about the half of it. I am sorry mom, and sorry I couldn't talk to dad. Tell him I love him."

"Sounds like we will never hear from you again."

"Don't be silly mom. Everything is going to be fine. Just remember to tell dad, and I love you too. Bye mom." Patrick ended the communication as he felt the lump forming in his throat. He knew he would never see her again. The pain building inside him, ripped at his emotions.

As he fell back into his chair, he leaned his head onto the headrest. He didn't have time to feel bad. His hurt would have to be pushed down, with so many other struggles he was having. As he spun around, he looked at his office. "So, I guess this will be my new home for now on."

Chapter 10 – Somewhere Out There

Patrick awoke to the blasting sound of the door of his office flying open. He jerked out of his seat. He had fallen asleep in his chair. He did not anticipate sleep at all. Somehow it came for him, in the night. In a way, he was grateful.

He stood up and shook off the aches that ran the course of his body, from the chair and sleeping in something other than his own bed. Making his way to the door, he staired into a glass on his wall and attempted to straighten his hair and clothes.

Turning to the door, he opened his mouth to say hello. "Well, Carter aren't you here early."

"Yes, but it is because you are not supposed to be here at all. I was contacted by an escort who is looking for you. Good thing is, I chipped you. So, this kind of situation would never be a problem."

"Wait, what do you mean you chipped me?" His expression totally changed.

"I loaded a tracking device into your body. That way, we never have to worry if you have been abducted, or worse." Carter answered him authoritatively.

"You chipped me?" He asked again. "You mean like they do to dogs and cats. I am a human; you just don't do that to a human."

"Calm down, it is for your own good."

"Calm down! You chipped me! How the hell did you accomplish this? I don't remember doing it." He ranted.

"I simply touched your shoulder. I had a medical device in my hand."

"You could have told me."

"Agreed, in the future, I will tell you, as I am injecting you."

"No, you will tell me before you put something into my person." He insisted.

"So, I should tell you of the nanobot injection as well?" She said smiling at him.

"What? How much have you done to me, that I am not aware of?"

"Nothing else…for the moment." She laughed

"No, nothing else without my consent. I am watching you now." He said turning away from her.

"Ok, but the escort is here to collect you. I will inform them that you are coming down to meet them."

"Ok, I will be ready in a minute. Just need to wake up. I can't believe I fell asleep here."

"About that, why did you?" Carter asked.

"I think I was just that exhausted."

"I understand. Maybe you will get more rest on your way to the space station." She tried to be supportive. "Oh, and Captain."

"Yes?"

"Be careful out there. We wouldn't want to lose you now. We need you back here soon."

"Thanks Carter, I will be out in a minute."

Patrick gathered a few of his personal belongings and threw them into his backpack. He was not sure what to take with him. The transport to the station would take over 24 hours. He grabbed his wrist communication device and headed for the door.

As he walked away, he looked around one last time. He was sure he would miss this place while he was gone. He was becoming accustomed to it. It was just as well, being he thought he would spend the rest of his life onboard.

As he met his transport, he climbed into the vehicle, and watched Discovery as he pulled away. It was finally a reality, and he admired the hard work everyone had put into it.

As he looked upwards, he could see the pods that were completely attached. The ship was massive from the outside, consisting of a long hull at the center which was comprised of several decks. Above, the pods sat two side by side, the whole length of the ship before coming to the bridge, which was large and half saucer shaped.

No earth ship had ever looked like this, or been as large. The government had cut funding to all things related to space, with the last of the Shuttle missions. Then scientists discovered that the environmental destruction was not reversable, and they scrambled to rebuild the remains of NASA. It was almost too late to make a difference.

As Patrick arrived at the shuttle launch pad, he stepped nervously from the car and began the journey to the door that awaited him. The idea of walking in space scared him, but he did not know why. In his mind, he was sure he would die.

He steadied himself and repeated that he was only being foolish. So many other astronauts had done spacewalks before. He was doing this with new technology, and men did this for over a hundred years. If he kept reassuring himself, he would be fine.

As the shuttle blasted skyward, Patrick held tight to the armrests of his seat. Leaning back, he cleared his mind of all things negative. He could not die on this journey, he had too many people depending on him. He was strong enough to do this.

Meanwhile, onboard the International Space Station, Pavel heard the all too familiar signal. He dreaded the message. He could not kill, not even on command. The message had few words, no video, it said plainly…" He is coming."

Chapter 11 – And So It Begins

As the final repairs to Discovery were being completed, an air of calm filled the ship. The crew were sure they had met their deadline. Carter walked across the bridge, observing each station. She took pride in her work. Trying hard not to get too confident, she held back the smile that was trying to cross her lips.

She turned to see the captain's chair. She had never considered her work would merit her such a title, but one day, she secretly hoped she would sit in the head position. As she walked in the direction, and staired down at it, the onboard alarm system began to screech through the calm atmosphere.

Turning to the communications officer she began to look concerned. "Is this another malfunction Jones?"

"No, the warning system went off because of an outside source. Wait, there is a message coming in from a secured government transmission."

"Put it on the main screen. I have a feeling we should all hear this one. Oh, and kill the noisemakers."

As the communications officer transferred the transmission, the blaring alarms silenced. Carter turned to see the official image of the government. It was real. Carter shook her head awaiting what she knew was bad news. Stephens came to her side and stood by her as the transmission opened.

"Carter, tell me that ship of yours is finished." The general said, with a grim look on his face.

"Ready enough for launch, if that is what you mean." She responded.

"Good, because you have a couple of hours at best. A nuclear warhead was loaded just minutes ago, and its intended target is the Discovery. We fortunately had an agent, who infiltrated the Russians. I say had, as soon as he notified us, he was killed. Get everything ready and get that ship off the ground."

"But sir, we have not readied the pods, there are no people transferred there yet." Carter sounded stressed as she tried to make him aware.

"Get them ready and active. After liftoff, transport them onboard. Fortunately, with the late hour, many will be asleep and will not be aware they have been relocated. If they are awake, stun them and make sure the information in the pods matches their histories. We need them calm, and having no knowledge of what has happened, until they are in space."

"General, this is such a gamble thinking that we can fool them."

"Carter, you are not fooling them. You are saving their lives."

"What about our captain? He is on the International Space Station."

"I am aware of the situation. You will have to pick him up in route. Get as close to the station as you can, and transport him, whether it is convenient or not. Understood?" The general growled.

"Understood sir. I will initiate a countdown, and finalize all loading. Sir, thank-you for this opportunity."

"No Carter, thank you…now make me proud and save our people."

"Will do." Carter turned from the screen as it went blank. "You heard the man, ready or not, we launch in an hour. I am not giving them time to blast our asses out of the sky."

Chapter 12 – Mass Destruction

Onboard the International Space Station, Pavel watched as the shuttle came along side and locked on. His heart beat quickly as he saw the American's enter the hatch. He watched them, carefully trying to figure out his target. Then he saw Patrick. 'Target acquired.' he thought to himself.

As Patrick came forward, he extended a hand to Pavel. As Pavel reached back, he studied the man. They were not enemies. In another place and time, they would have been friends. He ran it through his brain, how could he be forced to kill an innocent man?

The shuttle departed shortly after arriving, and Patrick prepared for his spacewalk. Fighting through his fear, he geared up with the help of Pavel.

Patrick did not hide his fear well, as he turned to face the Russian.

"Patrick, do you believe a man should follow orders from his government, even if it means going against his beliefs?" He said lowering his eyes.

"No way. You have to be true to yourself. After all, you have to look at yourself in the mirror, they don't."

"Really?" Pavel said low as he exhaled.

"What were you ordered to do?"

"Kill you, and leave your body in space."

"Well, if you are telling me, then you must not want to do this."

"They will kill me when I go home. I am a sitting bird."

Patrick laughed at him for a moment, "You mean sitting duck."

"Whatever the word, I will be dead."

"Then don't go home. Maybe we can arrange protection for you."

"You would do that?"

"Yes, that is who I am. Now, let's get this spacewalk over with, and figure out how I can help you."

~~~~~~

In the aftermath of the moon's explosions, a series of nuclear launches shot through the air on earth. Like a series of Dominoes, the nuclear sirens sounded in order of launch. There was no delay, each country's computers, readied themselves in retaliation.

The Discovery fired its engines, and moved skyward, as it prepared the populate its dome pods. Moving from one location to the next, they locked onto the individuals they had studied. In moments, they disappeared from their homes, beds or locations before reappearing in identical hologram generated environments.

"Carter, we have completed transfers, all is ready for departure." Stephens informed her.
~~~~~~

"Then I guess we need to find our captain. Ensign Jackson, set a course for the International Space Station. And People, take a moment and say goodbye to our former home and the ones we leave behind." She paused for a moment. "Let's do this."

As the huge ship lifted upwards, the engines left a trail across the sky. They were no longer a secret. Not that anyone would pay any mind with the outbreak of war.

Within hours they arrived, as Pavel watched out the window. "Patrick, you need to see this."

"What is it?"

"Something amazing." Pavel answered.

"Yes, it is. That is the Discovery. It is my ship, and if it is here, then things are worse than we could imagine."

"You Americans built that?"

"Yes." Patrick moved to the communications panel. "Carter, are you there."

"Yes, I am. Want a lift?"

"Yeah, and if you have room, I have a friend who would like to come too."

"Understood, engineering we have two ready to transport." Carter said smiling.

As Patrick and Pavel arrived on the bridge, the huge ship began moving past the space station. On the display screen, they saw the moon. The colonies were still lit, and it seems there was still life. They watched as the pieces of the moon separated and a huge section began to drift away from earth's gravity.

"What will happen to them?" Ensign Jackson asked.

"I don't know. The nuclear explosions acted as a propellant breaking them free. They will probably drift until they hit something or they find a way to control their drift. Whatever the case, I hope they survive. For now, there is nothing we can do to save them, or anyone we left behind." Patrick answered, as they all watched the view screen as it changed to the earth. There, nuclear explosions continued to light up the surface.

"I think it is time, we get the hell out of here." Carter added.

"You are right, ensign take us out, that a way." Patrick said as he turned and sat in his chair. "We have a planet to get to."

The following is a free excerpt from
G.W. Mullins' book

**Rise of The Snow Queen Book One
The Polar Bear King**

What begins as a simple, bittersweet tale about a man turned into a polar bear, grandly unfolds into a rich, mythical adventure, in this best-selling book series.

Based on Hans Christian Andersen's fairy tale, author G.W. Mullins expands on this classic story creating a new mythology that takes readers into the land of snow and ice.

G.W. Mullins

Rise Of The Snow Queen
Book Series

The Polar Bear King   War Of The Witches   The Story of Gerda and Kai

From the Author of the Best-Selling Novel Daniel Is Waiting
Rise of the Snow Queen
Book 1
Sometimes Fairy Tales Don't Have Happy Endings
The Polar Bear King
G.W. Mullins

**Rise of The Snow Queen Book One
The Polar Bear King**

**Is Available in Hardback (978-1-64008-096-6),
Paperback (978-1-64008-095-9) and various eBook
formats worldwide.**

Before

Jorgen gathered his climbing gear for early the next morning. He was determined to make his way to the mountain before the storm that was due later in the week. As he packed, his son Kristoffer watched intently, his eyes were filled with wonder and dreams of the climb. He wanted so badly to be at his father's side as he reached the top of the mountain.

"Papa, I want to go this year. I have practiced, I wouldn't be in your way." The boy pleaded.

"Kristoffer you are only nine. You would not be able to climb the rocks and hold the ropes as I do. I have told you many times when you are older, I will take you." Jorgen looked deep into his son's eyes and saw the hurt, but he knew there was no way he could take him. "Now off to bed with you, it is past your time, your mother will blame me for keeping you so late.

Jorgen ushered the boy to bed and then looked in on his daughter who slept in the next room. Gerda was sound asleep; she had no desire to climb mountains. Her life was filled with books and learning. He walked over to her bed and leaned in to kiss her on the forehead. She just curled up tighter and clung to her blanket. The fire in the house provided a barrier to the frozen valley around them, but when the wind blew, you could feel the house's every crack.

"Jorgen if you keep watching your daughter sleep, you will never get any sleep yourself." Freya whispered smiling at her husband.

"I know, sometimes I can't help myself, she reminds me so much of you. She'll break hearts one day, just like you did."

"I never set out to break hearts; I just captured the one I wanted. Now, if only I could convince you to stay home tomorrow. I don't want you to go."

She lowered her eyes so Jorgen could not see her pain.

"Freya, I have climbed so many mountains. I will be fine, you'll see."

Jorgen checked the house and made sure the fire would last as he headed to bed. Freya watched, unable to speak of the real feelings she had inside. She bore a secret that she dared not tell anyone not even her husband. She knew what was at the top of the mountain, but telling him might open up a bigger, more destructive secret. Silence was her only option for now and a hope he would not be able to reach the mountain peak or find the castle.

Freya did not sleep the entire night, she just lay there and watched Jorgen. She loved him more than anyone she had ever known. He was her family before the children came along. She had tried so hard to leave behind her birth family. Only her sisters remained, and she wanted nothing to do with them.

It had been nearly a decade since she left the mountain top and renounced her powers. She ran it all through her head over and over again. There had to be some fragment of her abilities left that could protect him on his journey. If she could only keep him from harm, she would use the power again.   As she looked over at the bedside table, she saw the broach. Her mother had given it to her as a girl. She treasured it; it was the only part of her past she allowed to remain.

As she held it in her hands, she ran her fingers over the rose flower shapes that made up its intricate design. "This will have to do." She whispered. Waving a hand over it, the familiar tingling ran through her fingers. A warm glow extended from her hand and engulfed the broach. The light was bright and red in color but it did not awake Jorgen. She smiled as she realized the power was still within her.

As she watched the power fill the broach, she whispered a spell of protection. And then she knew, she had accomplished her goal. Freya quietly slipped out of bed and went down to where her husband had left his equipment. As she looked it over, she saw the side pouch of his pack. It was there she hid his protector. She turned her head upwards, "Mother I promised I would never part with this, but I have to make sure he is safe. If you are watching, please make sure he comes back safely."

The morning came just as Freya finished her mission. She knew Jorgen would be up and leaving soon. As she went to the kitchen to prepare his food, her heart ached. This was wrong and she knew letting him leave, would not result in anything good. She also knew, she would not be able to stop him. When he made his mind up to do something, it could not be changed. This was the first time she wished she could.

Jorgen came down and ate as he watched Freya. He knew she was troubled but she would never tell him. He smiled at her as she walked past. As he extended a hand, she took it and looked him in the eyes. "I'll be alright." He tried to reassure her. It didn't work; she knew all too well how dangerous it was to go near the castle.

Jorgen started to leave for his climb when the sun was just up enough to see. He kissed Freya and waved good-bye. As he started his climb, he never looked back. His mission was to reach the top of the mountain before evening. He took the rugged rocks quickly and showed how his years of climbing made him an expert.

Stopping along the way to rest, he would look back and survey the valley below. More than once he was sure he saw something behind him, but after several hours he put it out of his mind. Maybe it was the altitude playing tricks with his mind. He stopped looking back by the afternoon, as he got to the high peaks. If he had looked back again, he might have seen his son Kristoffer making his way just minutes behind his father. The boy had been right; he was able to handle the climb.

The evening came and Jorgen reached the top of the mountain. He looked around him to take satisfaction in his accomplishment. It was then he saw it in the distance; a large structure of sleek and shimmering ice. It was a castle hidden at the very peak of the mountain, not visible to the valley below. He studied it as he walked the slope that led to the entrance.

The outside looked like an architectural dream. The walls surrounding the grounds were flawless. The gate was carved ice, as if done by a true craftsman. As he touched the gate it swung open effortlessly. Jorgen was hesitant about entering, he did not want to trespass, but he wondered who could live in a castle of ice. No human could exist there. He entered and walked through the middle of the garden. The flowers there were all made of ice resembling perfect delicate sculptures. No two were alike; they all had been carefully constructed to be flawless.

As Jorgen approached the steps to the huge doors that protected the front of the castle, he called out hello but no one answered. He continued to move up to a point that he could knock. As his hand touched the door it swung open. His heart almost stopped from fear of who or what might occupy the castle. His courage was not enough to take him inside. He backed down the steps where he originally came and to the side. Not realizing what he was doing, he stepped on one of the perfect flowers and it shattered.

The sound of the flower shattering rang throughout the mountain like a bell. Jorgen realized what he had done. He had to go in now and apologize. He just didn't know to whom. As he looked around, he did not notice that someone else had already become aware he was there. Far above on a balcony of the frozen castle, Elaida watched. She had created the gardens and the castle. Her eyes looked on, enraged as she watched her unwelcome visitor.

Kristoffer made his way to the gates of the castle, looking on in childlike amazement. He did not know things like this ever existed. He had never been taught it in school or dreamed it possible. He worked his way through the garden, as his father once again approached the door. Jorgen knocked again and when no response came, he stepped inside. Kristoffer was not far behind as he watched his father set down his pack by the door and walk to the large opening where a crystal looking staircase and chandelier engulfed the room.

Jorgen looked around at the decorations that adorned the hall. There were eleven statues made of ice that lined the walls. Each one was unique and carved with specific human features. All so lifelike and at the same time too perfect he thought. He had never seen such work in his life.

"Hello, is anyone here?" He called out and waited for an answer.

"And what do we have here?" A voice came from the top of the steps...

"I am sorry for the intrusion. I wanted to apologize for stepping on one of your flowers." Jorgen continued.

As the female walked down the steps Jorgen could see she was a beautiful woman with very white features and a long flowing sheer gown. Her eyes never left him, as she made her way down step by step. A sinister look covered her face. She looked at him as if she was a wild animal and he was her prey. She stopped several steps from the bottom landing. Elaida liked to be above the ones she spoke to; it gave her an air of power. That is also why the castle was located at the highest peak in the area.

"So, you destroyed one of my creations?" Elaida said lowering her head and glaring.

"I didn't mean to; I was backing down the steps and I stepped backwards onto one. I am so sorry I know these creations must be time consuming. They are so beautiful." He smiled at her.

"So, you like my work?" She spoke while looking at him with a psychotic expression.

"Yes, I especially like these statues. They are like nothing I have ever seen. How did you get the expressions so perfect?"

"Fear does a lot when someone is modeling for you. They just need motivation." She said as she descended the steps and began to walk circles around him.

"Why fear? What is there to be afraid of?" He asked.

"Well…me of course. Do you not find me frightening?" Elaida laughed out loud.

"No, you are very beautiful."

"Flattery… that could almost get you forgiven for destroying my work. You are quite a beautiful man. I have captured so many different looks and body types in my work, but never a man built like you. So many muscles and that handsome face. You could almost melt a girl's frozen heart." She spoke as she continued to walk around him running a fingertip over his chest.

"Thank-you I appreciate the compliments." Jorgen said uneasily.

"Not so much compliments, mostly me thinking out loud. I could use a new statue. It has been years since anyone made their way up the mountain. You must be quite the climber; the way is so icy and slick. But then it is supposed to be to keep prying eyes out of my castle."

Kristoffer listened intently trying to understand what was going on. The woman frightened him. She did not seem normal. Her skin looked as if it was made of ice. He managed his fear and waited to see what his father did.

"Do you live here alone?" Jorgen asked.

"Yes, I have for decades, since my parents died and my sisters went to their own domains."

"Aren't you lonely?"

"No, I have my friends here to keep me company."

"I am Jorgen, what is your name."

"My family called me Elaida. I have been known by many other names over the years. Maybe you have heard of me by reputation. How does the name Snedronningen strike you?"

"You are the Snow Queen?"

"Yes, I see you have heard of my bad reputation. People seem to misunderstand me so much; they have labeled me as frozen. I am so much more than that I am ice and destruction. I am a goddess. And you…are less than that."

Jorgen turned to look at the door. He was ready to run, but it was too late. The Snow Queen raised her hand and the ice entered through his feet. He couldn't move. Kristoffer looked on in fear at the fate of his father.

"You will be my latest masterpiece. I only had eleven before, now you complete my dozen. So handsome, I might have liked you, if my heart was not filled with ice. Now…join my collection."

Jorgen's whole body froze solid as his son watched. In a panic, Kristoffer stood up to run just as the Snow Queen spotted him. She turned loose a flurry of snow in his direction. Like a swarm of killer bees, they flew in his path like they had a mind and a purpose. As he ran, Kristoffer tripped over his father's pack and on the ground fell the broach his mother had put in. He knew what it was and picked it up as he scrambled to the door.

Just outside, the swarm of snow swirled around him. Kristoffer held tight to the broach as the bees touched his skin and piece by piece melted from the warmed air that surrounded him. The Snow Queen watched the magic taking place. "He has been charmed." She screamed. She recognized the broach and a rage soared through her.   Her sister was still alive.

Chapter 1: A New King on the Throne

The lands in the valley had always been prosperous and times were once good during the rule of the elder King Valeman. That was before the Witch became aware of the kingdom. As Prince Valeman was away in other parts, his father fell under her control. She warped his mind in a way he would only respond to her and obey her orders.

The kingdom fell into ruins under her control. The people suffered cruel and unusual punishment. The strain of the witch's power took a horrible toll on the Kings health. He did not live long after. The Queen sent out word by messenger to her son to return home and take his rightful place on the throne. Weeks passed but there was no sign of the prince. The Queen managed to rule in his absence but the state of the kingdom only worsened. When the prince did return home, there was little to return to.

As the Prince made his way to the home of his mother, he saw the destruction around them. He was heartbroken, not only for his father but his people as well.

"Mother how did this happen? How did everything fall apart like this?" The Prince pleaded for information.

"Your father was beguiled by the Witch from the North. She came here and befriended him. In doing so, she gained his trust and then she cast a spell on him to only trust her. She destroyed everything with her demands and abuse of the people." Queen Valeman lowered her head to hide her tears from her son.

"It's OK mother, I will make this right. The Witch will not find it so easy to control me."

The young Prince hugged his mother. He didn't know how, but he would save his people. But first, he had to lay his father to rest. He sent out word to all corners of the land that he was back and the funeral would be held immediately. People came from every village and town to say good-bye to the man they once loved. It all seemed so unreal that he could have been pushed over the edge both mentally and physically.

After the ceremony, the prince called upon all who had come, to return to the town center to participate in his coronation. The time for a new King, was well past due, he told them. Some were skeptical that he could undo the damage caused to them. Others were willing to believe in anything that freed them from the Witch's power.

As the crown was placed on the head of the new King, the crowds cheered. There was a feeling of release and hope. In all the excitement, no one witnessed the Witch who was looking on from the trees nearby. Many did however notice the cold air that swirled down the hill. As she watched, the Witch stared intently at the new King. She studied his handsome face and chiseled jaw line. She admired his blond hair, cut ever so shortly and the muscles throughout his body. 'He would make a fine husband.' She thought.

She hid behind the guise of an old woman as she made her way near him. As she passed through the crowd, she seemed pleased with herself that it all came so easily. 'If they only knew the Snow Queen was this close to them, they would run and hide in their trashy hovels.' She thought to herself. She walked all the way up to the King with no resistance.

Pleased with herself for getting as far as she did, she knew she still had to get him alone. As she passed by the platform he stood on, she greeted him and just as he extended his hand to her, she fell to the ground. She seemed helpless and ill. Just as she had hoped, the ruse worked, for the King ordered two of his men to escort her to his private chamber to rest and have water. As the King arrived and his men left, the old woman stood up.

The King stepped back in shock; he did not understand. Then the old woman transformed into her true self. The rags she wore fell to the ground and she stepped forward in a beautiful gown and revealed herself as the Snow Queen. The King studied her for a moment and then realized she was the witch everyone spoke of.

"So, you are the one who corrupted my father and destroyed the kingdom? Valeman leered at her.

"Destroyed…is such a harsh word. Maybe we should say I used the Kingdom for my own benefit." She laughed evilly as she stared him in the eyes.

"So, you think it is Ok to just show up one day and plunder what is not yours?"

"If it suits my purposes…why not?" She studied him intently looking for his weaknesses.

"Your time here is done. I am in charge now and it's your time to leave."

The Snow Queen laughed out loud, "You just don't know what I am capable of. Push me again…and you will find out the hard way."

"What do you want? There isn't anything here anymore that you can take, the land is barren, there is no fortune to be found. The people have nothing."

"I wouldn't say there isn't anything I could want." She spoke in a sexy voice, as she walked around his back running her hand over his shoulders.

The king felt the chill run through his bones. He realized then, why she was called Snow Queen. His heart sank as he finally began to understand her desires. She wanted to be a Queen to his King. A merging of the two of them, to create a master kingdom. With him at her side, she knew they could conquer any enemy.

"There would be no kingdom that could defeat my frozen army of ice warriors and polar bears."

"You are crazy, we are a peaceful people. We do not war against those around us. We work to better ourselves and our friends." The King insisted.

"Your father understood my desires. It was easy to sway him; I could show you how I did it. You might even enjoy it." She whispered in his ear as he tried to resist her advances. "Now, be a good boy and I will make you very happy."

"Not a chance in hell, I will never marry you and you will never control this land again!"

"Never say never…sweetheart! I tried to do this the easy way, and you just had to be a bad boy. Now…suffer at the hands of a true Queen. By light one way, by night another. Your form will change, you will soon discover. By day a beast of a bear you will be, at night a man while others sleep. To break this spell you must achieve, the love of another while being the beast." She clapped her hands as she finished the spell sealing his fate. "Now go and find true love, if you can, and if for seven years after you find this love the person does not look upon your human form you will be a man only. If they do look upon you as a man, you are mine to take."

"What did you do to me? What does all of this mean?" He demanded answers.

"It means my darling handsome boy, when you come to your senses and agree to marry me the spell will be ended. If you do not, for the next seven years by day you will be a smelly…nasty…polar bear. At night…you will be a man. If you can find someone to love you as a bear, then in seven years you are your old self again. The spell will end. It's not hard to understand. Now, wouldn't it just be so easy for you to change your mind?"

The King looked at her in disbelief. "You can't just make me change into a polar bear. It's not possible."

"Want to bet on that one? I have so many powers you would not believe. I can create ice and snow, I can cast spells to get things I want, and I can even damage your life more than you could ever imagine possible." With her last words, the expression on her face changed completely to rage. She knew she was not going to win this fight.

She backed up a few steps as she stared hard at the King. He felt a strange sensation in his hands. His fingernails began to darken and white hair started to sprout out of his skin. His face stretched and distorted, as did much of his body, as he let out a blood curdling scream. As he fell to the floor, his body mass increased and his clothes ripped away. He rolled over face down as his body transformed completely into a bear.

As he rose up, the remnants of a human male were gone. He was now a beast. He turned to the Snow Queen, and in a rage prepared to rip her limb from limb.

"Now…now, temper will get you nowhere. And if you kill me, you will still be under my spell for seven years. Now don't you think you should be a good boy and change your mind?"

The King growled loudly, sounding like a tormented animal. He knew he could not give in. He would have to find another way to break the spell. He turned, as if to aggressively rush at the Snow Queen, but she blew the full force of a winter storm in his direction and he fell to the floor.

"Nice try my love, but you will have to be faster than that to get to me." She walked over to him and formed an ice block to hold his feet together. "I think it is time for me to leave. A girl has to take care of herself, and you seem a little too hostile right now. I'll give you some time to think about your future, then we will talk again. Just…stay cool until then. "She laughed as she left the palace and the Polar Bear King.

Chapter 2: Rise of the Polar Bear King

King Valeman sat upon the floor of his chamber. He still could not believe what had happened to him. He shook his huge white head back and forth. His actions were still clumsy; he was not used to his new form. He tried to stand up and was wobbly at first. When he learned to stand on all fours it came easier to him.

"This was easier when I was pissed off." He growled in his deep throated voice.

He walked over to the dressing mirror and stared at his appearance. He had really transformed to a large white bear, there was no denying it. His mind raced, trying to conceive some way of returning to his former self. He did not know magic or anyone who could perform such acts of this level. His only chance for living a normal life was to find love and wait seven years.

Since no one knew of what happened, he stood behind his door and called out for a servant to bring his mother. He knew this would not be easy. If he stayed hidden while he talked to her, she may just believe it was him in the form of the bear. There was no other way. One thing he knew for sure, he would have to leave the palace and the kingdom, without anyone knowing he had changed.

His mother arrived and upon entering the room called out for him. From behind a dressing blind, he spoke to her.

"Mother, I need to tell you something, and you need to understand what I am telling you is truth. Do you understand?" He asked her.

"Yes, my son, I trust you. Tell me what is wrong?"

"The witch came back. She demanded I marry her. I refused and she put an enchantment upon me.

I am no longer as I was." His voice trailed off in a scratchy gruff tone.

"What did she do to you? What has happened to your voice?" The Queen became terrified.

"She cursed me to be in the form of a Polar Bear, if I find true love after seven years, I will return to being a man. If not, I will be this way forever. Mother, I have to leave here and go far away to resolve this. It is too soon after father's passing for the people to endure this. If the kingdom is to survive, I must leave for a time. You can rule in my absence. Since the witch is no longer here you will be able to rebuild what was destroyed."

Valeman's heart sank as he told his mother of his plans. He knew the task he had burdened her with was great, but he had no choice. It would be dangerous to have him stay there. His mother bowed her head down as tears ran from her cheeks. It was too much too soon; she had just laid her husband to rest and then to have to lose her son so quickly was insane.

As she cried, Valeman could not stand the pain he heard. He walked out from behind his hiding place and the Queen looked up and screamed. She was terrified at the sight before her. Her son really had been changed but she was not prepared.

"Mother please, it is still me in here…just changed."

"You are a beast, a great white bear. I am sorry; I was not prepared for the site of this."

"I know mother, and imagine what our people would say if they were to see it. I cannot rebuild the kingdom if the people fear me or just see me as the Polar Bear King. I do not want to rule a people in fear of me. I must go for a time, but I will return when I find a solution to this."

"Where will you go my son? Where will you be safe?" The Queen became scared for his safety.

"I don't know. I guess I will have to travel to the Winterland, the Kingdom of Ice and Snow. It would seem the appropriate place for a bear such as me."

He drew a deep breath and sighed. There really were not very many other options but to leave everything he knew behind. He told his mother he would leave that evening. It would be easiest then, since he would return to human form and be able to leave the palace without arousing suspicion. He felt a lump in his throat, for he knew after this, he would never be the same again.

As night spread across the land, he looked out upon the balcony. The rays of the moon shone in, and as one hit his paw, the transformation began. "By light one way, by night another." He whispered the words as he transformed into the man he had once been. As the moonlight coated his body, he stood there naked by the balcony. He looked at his skin and remembered what it was like to be a human.

He walked to the mirror and stood there. His mind raced over what had happened and he wondered for a moment should he have given in to the Snow Queen. All would be resolved if he did. As he stood there thinking, he did not notice the snowflakes which began to fall on the balcony or the approach of the woman who came with them.

"I think I like you just as much with your clothes off." The Snow Queen laughed.

"Don't get used to it. This is as close as you will ever get to me naked in a bed chamber." The King snarled as he tried to conceal his nakedness.

"Ha, don't be ashamed sweetheart, I am actually impressed. You have nothing to be embarrassed about."

"Why have you come back? Did you feel the need to ridicule me?"

"No, I thought you might want to reconsider your position."

"Go to hell witch." He screamed at her.

The Snow Queen lowered her head as she looked at him with rage in her eyes and screamed, "Don't call me a witch, I am so much more than that. I am Ice, I am Snow, I am a Goddess to be worshipped. And you are nothing more than a Polar

Bear King. And that you shall stay until the enchantment has run its course."

The Snow Queen turned and walked towards the open balcony doors. As she stepped out, she turned and looked at him one last time. "Such a pity, we could have had so much fun together. Now, the time for fun is over. I think you need to learn how to suffer." With her last words, she rose off the balcony, boarded her ice craft and flew off into the night leaving a trail of frost on the ground below her.

The King dressed and gathered a few things he could take in a pack with him for the journey. His mother returned to see her son off. She placed a chain around his neck that her husband had given to her as a memento of love and protection. Her son had only returned and now she had to say good-bye again. She knew it had to happen. There was no chance for him if he stayed. The King walked down the steps of the palace and climbed on the back of his horse. He rode as fast as he could to the edge of the land and it was there, he dismounted. He patted the loyal horse on its back and told it to return home. "The rest of this journey…I go on alone."

Included next are the first chapters of G.W. Mullins' Best-Selling title

Rise of The DarkLighter Book One
Dark Awakening

From the Author of the Best-Selling
Book Series "From The Dead Of Night"
Rise of the Darklighter
Book One
Dark Awakening
To fight evil, you have to embrace the darkness.
G.W. Mullins

Rise Of The Dark-Lighter Book One

Dark Awakening

Is Available in Hardback (978-1-64871-256-2), Paperback (978-1-64871-159-6) and various eBook formats worldwide.

Nuestra Señora de la Santa Muerte, also known as Santa Muerte, is an idol, female deity or folk saint in Mexican and Mexican-American Catholicism. The personification of death, she is believed to be associated with healing, protection, and delivering her devotees safely into the afterlife. Many consider her an angel of death.

Before

The lightning struck around them, as Malachi struggled to steer the car through the debris that the storm threw in their way. His heart raced and he could feel the pounding in his chest. He was scared, probably more scared than he had ever been before. For once in his self-absorbed life, this was not about him, a life was on the line.

"Hang on Uncle, I am doing my best to get us to the hospital. The storm is not making this easy." Malachi tried to comfort him.

"I know, I am holding on. You know I never said how proud I am of you." Carl's voice trailed off into a cough.

"Be still Uncle. There will be time for that after I get you to the hospital."

As Malachi spoke, he attempted to wipe the condensation from the windshield of the car. His efforts were in vain, as he would finish wiping, the fogginess would return. The car was old and barely drivable, it should not have been on the road, but in this situation, he had no choice.

As Malachi looked away to slap his hand against the defroster, he took his eyes off the road. It was then the storm took its vengeance and a funnel cloud passed in front of them. As its winds ripped through the road, a huge oak tree began to sway. Malachi looked up just in time to see it uprooted and flying towards the car.

Malachi let out a scream, as he knew there was nothing he could do to get out of the tree's path. As the tree hit the front grill of the car, it spun out of control and rolled down the deserted street. Flipping end over end, the crushed vehicle landed at the white picket fence that surrounded a country church.

As he looked out through the broken windshield, Malachi felt the blood running down his forehead. Struggling to lift his arm to his head, he felt the pain of being thrown around the vehicle in the crash. He was not sure, but the pain in his chest felt like a cracked rib. The pain came in jabs with his every movement. At first, he did not think of his uncle, then the realization hit him, he was not hearing any noise from the back seat.

Malachi turned to look around. A feeling of dread washed over him. How could his uncle have survived? The man was at death's door before the crash. Looking to the backseat, there was nothing. He was alone in the car.

Looking up through the broken glass, he scanned the road, until he found the form of a body laying several feet behind. His heart sank as he assumed the worst. He had failed with is most important thing he had ever had to do. Pushing against the seat, Malachi attempted to move his battered body to the driver's side door. He pulled the handle and leaned in, but the door was bent and mangled.

Leaning back, Malachi pulled his legs to his chest. He felt the surge of pain as he tried to hold them back with his arms. With all the energy he could muster, he let loose and kicked the door. It flew open quickly, and with such a force, that it slammed into the fender and then to the ground.

Malachi crawled out of the opening and fell to his knees. His head spun around, as dizziness overtook him. The rain blasted all around, as he tried to look towards his uncle. With every drop that hit his head, the blood that covered him splattered and ran down his face. It was no time, before his entire face was covered in red. His eyes stung and burned as he tried to focus, and began to try to get to his feet.

He wobbled back and forth, and lost his footing, falling to the ground as soon as he stood up. He was determined. His mind raced and his life flashed before him. He had accomplished nothing in the twenty years he had been alive. His past was a blur of selfishness and a desire to acquire money.

As he slammed into the paved road, his parent's faces ran through his mind. He wondered if they would have been ashamed of him. He never considered it before. They died when he was very young. He barely knew them. It was then his uncle Carl came and took him in. Malachi felt tears welling in his burning eyes, as he realized the only person on earth that cared for him, was just a few feet away and dying.

Malachi pushed his hands onto the pavement and forced himself upwards. Crawling at first, he finally got his footing and made his way to the lifeless body he saw before him. He fell to his knees at Carl's side and screamed out.

"Be still young one, I am not dead yet." A quiet shaky voice came from Carl's lips.

"Uncle, you are alive. I thought you were…"

"Dead…you can say the word. We all must die sometime, just not this minute. Perhaps soon though." Carl began to cough with his last words.

"No, I will get you help. I promise you I will."

"Malachi, just calm yourself. Go to the church and see if anyone is there. If the priest is in, get him to come and bring me inside."

Malachi rose to his feet, and moved as quickly as he could, to the church doors. As he pulled at the handles, the doors did not move. They were locked. Malachi knew he had to find a way to get his uncle out of the storm. He drew back his fists and threw them at the red wooden door. He screamed out, as he beat on the wood, and threw himself against it trying to force his way in. Just as he was about to give up, the door opened.

"What is happening here?" Father Timothy said hastily as he looked down and saw the bloody face of Malachi. "What has happened to you my boy?"

"The storm, it caused the car to crash and my uncle is badly hurt."

"Why would you come out in a mess like this anyway?" The priest asked.

"My uncle was ill before we left, I think he is dying. Please, can you help him?"

The two made their way to Carl, who was passing in and out of consciousness. Father Timothy took hold of him, and Malachi assisted as they lifted Carl from the ground. The rain pounded down heavily upon them, as they made their way to the door of the church.

Safely inside, they laid Carl's limp body on a pew, near the front of the chapel. Carl's lips moved as if he was speaking to someone. Malachi was not sure of who, he was not sure he wanted to know. He was only sure he was more scared than he had ever been. He looked down at his hands, as they shook uncontrollably. He tried not to succumb to his fears.

The priest returned with towels and a cup of hot tea. As he reached down to Malachi, the boy just looked up to him, barely able to form words. Taking the drink, Malachi held it in his hands, warming them as the priest began to wipe the blood from his forehead and face. Malachi smiled at him trying to find the strength to say thank-you.

"Your uncle needs help that I cannot provide. I can take care of the spiritual end, but honestly, that will not save him. He needs a doctor and medicine. From the looks of him, he was having a heart attack, long before you came out into the storm." Father Timothy said as he continued to clean Malachi's wounds.

"How do we get a doctor? The storm is worse than before. I cannot go anywhere without a car." The boy said, as he hung his head.

"You cannot go anywhere regardless, you are injured. The storm is no place for you in your condition. I will go. I know the roads, and a few shortcuts."

"But how will you get there? You can't walk in this storm."

"I have a motorcycle. It was donated to the church years ago. and I have become very good at riding it. Don't look at me like that, I might be a priest, but I can do normal things you know. Stay here and watch over your uncle. I will be back as soon as I can."

"Father, please be careful. Oh, and thank-you for what you are about to do."

Timothy acknowledged him, and turned to go. Malachi admired his bravery. He wished he was braver than he was. He returned to his uncle's side looking down at him. Carl was still moving his mouth as if he were speaking. The words were not intelligible, but still he spoke under his breath.

As Malachi watched, his uncle's eyes flew open and he pulled his arms close to his chest. Calling out, his voice began to make sense, and his words were clearer. He looked to Malachi and stretched out an arm to grab at him.

Malachi went down on his knees and took his uncle's hand. "What is it uncle. Are you feeling better?"

"No, my boy, I am fighting. The demons of death are coming for me. I need help to fight them. I need you to pray for me. Pray to Santa Muerte, ask her to help me. She will come."

"Uncle, she is not real, she is only a myth. Old Spanish women prey to her as a way to escape their unhappiness." Malachi insisted.

"She is not a myth, she is real. I have known many who have seen her, she comes when life is about to end. She can save me. Please do this for me. You must give her an offering. Place a bowl of water at the alter and pray to her."

"I do not believe in this or in religion, but if it will calm you, I will do it. Now rest as I go find water."

As Malachi searched through the building, he found the kitchen and a bowl for the water. As he filled it, he shook his head, not believing he was about to participate in this craziness. In his heart he knew he had to do it, if for no other reason, to calm his uncle until help came.

Malachi returned to the chapel and placed the water near a statue and cross, in the front of the room. As he kneeled on the floor, he looked up at the Virgin Mary. He wished he believed, in this religion, or in anything that would help them. His heart was too cold and barren he thought.

As he bowed his head, he began to ask for help from Santa Muerte. He asked her to come to him, to aid him in the saving of his uncle. He offered her the bowl of water as an act of respect. Then he closed his eyes. He called for help, and the darkness answered back.

The light in the room faded, as a shadow came forward from the darkened back wall. The figure of a woman took shape. She had dark features and her head was bowed. As she slowly walked forward, Malachi looked up. He prepared to scream, as she raised a shriveled finger to her dried lips.

As he looked at her, he could make out her face, it was drawn and looked as if she had been dead. She retained the features of a woman, but was as much skeleton as human. Her skin looked as if it had been wrapped around bone with no real meat left to her body. Malachi was scared, and his heart raced as she slowly moved towards him.

As she came in his direction, Malachi fell backwards from the feet of the statue. He scrambled trying to get upright. A scream became trapped in his lips as he crawled to the side of his uncle.

Leaning down, Santa Muerte picked up the bowl of water. She moved it to her leathery looking lips and allowed the water to pass into her mouth. She drank until the water was gone. Then she sat the bowl back down and turned towards them.

Malachi stared at her, as she began to smile. As he looked, her appearance began to change. With every second, she became more human in appearance. Her skeletal structure became more flesh-like. Her body filled out, and her face became normal. She laughed out-loud as the transformation became complete.

"Your offering is accepted. I needed that.
But why have you disturbed my sleep. It has been
many years since I graced this plane. No one has
called out to me in over a decade." Santa Muerte
looked at him inquisitively.

"My uncle, he is ill. I fear he is dying. Please
save him." Malachi pleaded with her.

Extending a hand, she reached down and
touched Carl's head. She smiled at him as Carl
looked back to her. A joy rushed over him as he saw
that Malachi had done as he asked. Carl sat up as
Santa Muerte cradled him in her arms.

"Your time to leave this plane was not meant
to be as of yet." She spoke softly.

"What do you mean? Is he not dying?"

"That is not what I meant. He was not
supposed to die for some time yet. His fate has
changed."

"Can you save him?" Malachi pleaded for
answers.

"It does not work that way ignorant boy. Life cannot just be given. It is an exchange. A life for a life. One forfeits, so another may live. For him to continue in this existence, another must take his place in death. Now that wouldn't be fair, would it boy?" She asked him.

"No, but I do not want him to die. You have to save him."

"Not everything is by your human choosing. If he is to live, then you tell me whose life to claim in his place. Would you choose that I take the life of the priest that left here unselfishly trying to save another, or perhaps another innocent who does not even know you. Or perhaps, you are willing to exchange your life for his?" She laughed out hysterically, as she walked around looking at the statues in the church.

"No, this cannot be. Malachi, do not even consider her offer. If this is the only way, then I choose death. Take me now Angel of Death. I believed in you and what you stand for. I had no idea you were so cruel and heartless." Carl screamed at her.

"Heartless," she laughed. "I am here to save you, and you call me heartless. I should strike you down myself for your disrespect. I was human like you, and I know the pain of death. You lived much longer than I did. Do not whine to me about your pathetic life. If you want to live, a choice must be made."

"Is there no other way?" Malachi pleaded with her.

"Perhaps, there is. I tire of coming here to this existence to take lives. Become my apprentice, help in my work. Then in the time of one year, you can win back your freedom, if you fulfill your duties."

"You mean, I would not die, and I can come back to my life."

"As pathetic as it is. Yes, you can return, but only at a time I agree. Your Uncle will live, and may do so until his actual time of death that was ordained."

"Then I agree to your terms." Malachi choked on his words.

"No, Malachi do not let her take you. She will not honor the deal. Run from here." Carl screamed.

"It is too late old man, I have him now. The deal is struck. He is mine."

As she turned to look back at Carl, she reached out a hand and Malachi took it. As they walked towards the back hall of the church, they both faded into darkness. Carl stood up, feeling the energy flowing through him again. He was healed, and his life returned. Malachi was not so lucky.

Chapter 1 - Out of The Past

Santa Muerte stood looking, through her portal into the past. She thought about her new apprentice. She watched as he slept. Her mind raced to when she was still human. Moving her hand over the portal, she saw the mist change within, the images went back to the time of 1847. The Mexican-American war raged through Texas. She stared on until she saw herself.

She clung to her mother, as they made their way through the side street trying to avoid the spray of bullets. Her mother pulled her close. Fear covered her face; she had no idea how to save them. They were surrounded by the fighting.

As her mother pulled her into the shelter at the end of the house, Anna looked up to her. She did not understand what was happening. Her mother clung to her trying to quiet her cries.

"Anna…" Her mother spoke. Santa Muerte played the moment over and over again. It had been so long since she had heard her own name said, or her mother's voice saying it. Her cold heart throbbed in her chest. She wasn't supposed to feel this way anymore. She had given up feeling anything about life or people years ago. It was too much of a toll on her. When she inherited her role as an angel of death, she left so much behind.

Looking back into the past, she watched her mother as she cared for Anna who was only six. This war was no place for her. Children were supposed to be carefree and happy. She should have been playing somewhere in a field of flowers. Instead, she was facing an army of soldiers. Santa Muerte glanced down for a moment, she knew what was coming, and that much could still hurt her.

"Mi amor, I promise this is not what I planned for you in life. Please, no matter what happens, remember mama loved you so much. If I could have changed this, I would have. I just do not know how to save you or myself."

As Carlotta finished speaking, she heard the soldiers making their way down the side street. She pulled Anna close and covered her mouth. "Do not cry, do not make a sound." She whispered, as the door began to open slowly. Carlotta raised her head as she came eye to eye with the enemy she had come to fear.

"Stand up woman." He screamed at her.

"Please, I beg of you, spare my child." She cried out.

As the soldier studied her, he did not care for her or her child. He raised his rifle into the air. A smile crossed his lips, as he prepared to claim another notch for his collection of kills. The shot rang out, as Anna watched her mother fall sideways on the ground.

Anna screamed and grabbed at her mother. She pulled at Carlotta's hand, but she did not move.

Anna struggled to arouse her mother, it was no use, she was gone. The young girl had no concept of death or murder. In that day, she witnessed both within minutes. She stood looking at her mother and screaming, as the soldier reloaded his rifle.

"Looks like my lucky day, two Mexicans at the same time. Don't worry, it will be over soon." He said laughing at Anna.

She stood there watching, paralyzed by her own fear. Santa Muerte yelled at her, "Why don't you run and hide. Just save yourself." She raised her hands to her head, as the sound of the rifle firing, rang through the room. Clutching her chest, she caressed the point where the bullet had hit her. If she still had a heart, she thought it would hurt.

Her eyes filled with tears as she watched. The soldier left, walking away proud of himself and his deeds. She felt hatred filling her. She grinned, and thought to herself, there must still be some emotions left inside somewhere. As the killer turned to leave the alley, a Mexican soldier came from around the corner and fired before he was seen. The murderer fell to the ground, a grim look on his face. As he looked up, he saw the dark one coming for him.

A few feet away, the dark shadow came. As it moved forward, it took shape. A man emerged from within the darkness. Dressed in black from head to toe, he wore a dress suit and looked like an undertaker. Looking about, the dark one studied the area. "So many dead, so many souls to claim. I'll be here a while." The Angel of Death was pleased.

He cleared the street of the dead before surveying the area. He made his way down the street until finding the bodies of Carlotta and Anna. Looking down at Anna, he shook his head. "Little One, you never had a chance in life, did you?"

As he lifted Anna into his arms, he carried her through the streets. His pain was obvious, as he struck out at those who caused the death of such a young girl. In moments, he killed all who were in the immediate area, before lifting himself upwards with the child still in his arms.

In his own realm, he took Anna to his private chamber. There he took a small amount of his power and formed a ball of energy in front of him. Looking down at the girl, he aimed his hand, shooting the power within her. "My child, forgive me for what I do, but this is the only way I know to give you life again." With the power surging through her, she took a deep breath, and sat up coughing.

"Arise Muerte. My child, born of death."

"My name is Anna, she said staring at him."

"You were Anna, now you are so much more. You are Queen of the Dead."

"I don't understand." She questioned him.

"In time, it will all make sense to you. But for now, you will grow and learn."

As his words echoed through the room, Malachi watched from behind. He had been watching the whole time. He understood a little better what was happening. He had enlisted his soul with that of the dead.

Included next are the first chapters of G.W. Mullins' Best-Selling title

**From The Dead Of Night Book One –
Daniel Is Waiting**

From
The
Dead
Of
Night
Book Series

Death is only the beginning.
Daniel walked in the land of the Dead.
Now the Dead want him back

Daniel Is Waiting

Daniel Returns

Daniel Awakens

Daniel's Fate

GW
Mullins

From The Dead Of Night Book One
Extended Anniversary Edition
Death is only the beginning
Daniel Is Waiting
A Ghost Story
G.W. Mullins

From The Dead Of Night Book One –
Daniel Is Waiting

Is Available in Hardback (978-1-64516-874-4),
Paperback (978-1-64516-873-7) and various eBook
formats worldwide.

ghost

gōst/

noun

noun: ghost; plural noun: ghosts

1.   an apparition of a dead person that is believed to appear or become manifest to the living, typically as a nebulous image.

"the building is haunted by the ghost of a nun"

synonyms: specter, phantom, wraith, spirit, presence

Sixty Years Ago

"Mom why are you being so crazy about this? I just want to know the truth." Daniel pleaded with Emily, but she became more outraged. The final threads of the lie she and her husband had hidden for sixteen years was unraveling. Daniel had stumbled onto the truth. Being a head strong teenager meant he was not going to give up easily and let it rest.

"Daniel, sometimes the past is better left in the past. Why won't you just leave this all alone before you cause more problems than ever imagined." Emily pleaded with him.

"No, I want the truth. Is the woman I saw with dad, my mother, or are you. I am tired of being lied to. I have felt my whole life something was wrong. I don't know how but I have always known, didn't you see how as a child I would never call you Mommy? Damn-it, tell me the truth."

"Ok, you want the truth, then I will give it to you. You are not my son. You are the bastard child of my husband and his secretary. While I was home being the loving and devoted wife, your dad was out screwing around. He thought he wouldn't get caught. Well guess what, when you get another woman pregnant, then you get caught. At least my children will be born into a house of marriage." Emily spewed forth all the hatred she had pushed down for so long.

She reveled in delight as she unloaded years of pain and hatred. She never thought about the fact it was aimed at the wrong person. Emily's husband should have been her target, instead of an innocent sixteen-year-old boy, who bore the load of his father's sin.

Daniel stared on in disbelief as he tried to conceive how such a thing could be true. The man he had loved and respected his whole life had been living a lie. And what was worse, he had made Daniel live that lie as well. His whole world began to crash around him. Nothing and no one he ever believed in was real anymore. They were just a group of actors, each one playing the roles they assigned themselves.

A tear ran down Daniel's face as he looked into Emily's eyes. She was as much a victim as he was. Confusion filled his mind as he searched for any clear way to accept any of it. All he knew was that he wanted to get out of the house of lies that was closing in around him. He turned and headed for the door as a look of terror crept across Emily's face. Her only thought was. 'What have I done?'

Daniel raced for the door before Emily could plead with him not to go. She knew what she had done was wrong. She knew when James came home from work, there would be hell to pay for this. She had to fix the mess she had made. She had to keep Daniel at home and persuade him not to tell his father what he found out.

Emily raced for the door and grabbed her keys. Daniel had to be nearby, there wasn't enough time for him to get far. As she raised the garage door, the rain poured on her head. She worked quickly to get down the drive, but in her confusion, she backed the car into the side porch before squealing tires and heading for the main road.

As she drove, the rain pelted her windshield. The old wipers were too shredded to keep the window clear. Emily could barely see as the tears burned her eyes and the windshield started to fog over. Rounding the corner, she didn't see Daniel walking by the road. As she tried to wipe the windshield, the car swerved towards the edge.

Daniel heard the sound of the car coming at him, but it was too late to move. He looked into the headlight's bright white glow as the car ran him down. As he fell to the ground unconscious, his last thoughts were almost humorous. He started life as an accident and now he would die that same way.

Emily jumped from the car and frantically ran to his side. Time stopped for her in that moment. Everything around her froze as she felt the pain hit her heart so hard it was as if it was going to explode. She screamed out for help, hoping someone, anyone would hear her. She just sat there in her frozen state cradling Daniel in her arms. She only whispered in Daniel's ear, "I am so sorry…I was wrong."

~

Daniel was rushed to the hospital in a comatose state. Days and weeks went by but there was no change in his condition. Visitors came and went, but one regular guest was always present…Janet Blakely. She had allowed Daniel's father to take him from her at birth, she wasn't going to allow the same thing in death. She cared for Daniel just as if he was a small child. She read to him, told him stories about her life and shared her dreams of what he would become. In the matter of a few short weeks, she shared a lifetime with him. And in the end, she shared his death.

Daniel died peacefully. His mother sitting beside him stroking his short dark blond hair. A lump rose up in her throat as she realized he wasn't breathing. Janet called for the doctor's, but there was nothing they could do. They only told her, he had gone to a better place. She looked at the doctors in a blind rage wondering how anyone would think of death as being a better alternative to life.

Janet walked to Daniel's bed as the doctors and nurses left. Taking his hand, she said her goodbyes as her heart filled with regret. Maybe if she had not given him up, he would still be alive. As she released his hand, she removed the ring he was wearing. It was a class ring with a brilliant blue stone. She held it close to her heart and cried, as the nurse came to escort her out.

When Janet got home, she placed the ring in her jewelry box. She had to put her secret to rest. If her husband found out, she knew he would leave. A hidden part of her life was over. Her last act before she closed the jewelry box, was to phone the local paper and place an obituary for her son Daniel Blakely. As the call ended, the lid of the jewelry box closed and its rhythmic music ended.

~

At the funeral home the next day James and Emily viewed the body of their son for the last time. James had not let go of his anger, it had only mixed with his grief and made him intolerable at times. As James looked at the remains of his son, he noticed the school ring was missing from Daniel's hand. He flew into a rage questioning the director of the funeral home, but he was told there never had been a ring and it probably didn't make it from the hospital.

As they approved the casket and the body, the lid was closed. Daniel's body was laid to rest the next day. It should have been an ending to a very unfortunate destructive situation. It was not. Death is an unexplainable mystery. We think of life and death by human terms. But the dead have another existence all their own. Sometimes, death is only the beginning.

As the crowds died down and the mourners left the graveside, there was a stillness in the air. The family car pulled away passing Janet as she watched from a distance. The casket was placed into the mausoleum, as a breeze swept across the cemetery grounds. It swirled and kicked up leaves and debris. In the center of the whirlwind formed a blue light. The light grew brighter and larger unseen to anyone in the area that was living. The dead however, watched intently to see what was happening. As the light formed a long shaft, a form emerged taking the shape of a young blond-haired man.

The light dissipated as Daniel opened his eyes and reached his hand to his head. The feeling was like he had a head ache. He was groggy and hung over. He looked around at the tombstones and shook his head wondering how he had gotten there. He was confused but who wouldn't be when waking up dead?

Mass Destruction

Today

"I'm worried about you Jen. What will you do when I am gone? "She hadn't thought much about it.

"You can't stay here by yourself. It's not safe. I mean, when there were more of us kids at home, then we could help each other when they would fight. You don't stand a chance by yourself."

"Aww Jay.... you know me, I can always find a place to hide."

"Like where?"

"Maybe the attic" Jen laughed. She knew Jay was aware she was terrified of the attic and the possibility of mice.

"You have to think this out before I go. It's not safe with mom and dad's fighting and it's not safe on the streets with the gangs roaming the area."

Jen knew she was in a bad situation and there was no time for joking. She also knew if she didn't convince Jay she would be OK, that he wouldn't leave for school. He had worked too hard to get in there, and she couldn't ruin it for him.

"I can always stay with friends," Jen said unconvincingly. She knew this wasn't a solution, she had just a couple of good friends and their parents would get suspicious if she was there too much. Deep inside she wished she was going off to school too. Away from her parent's constant arguing and the violence that often followed.

Jen thought about her parents and how with all the other kids gone, everything would fall on her. Her mom had depended on Jay for everything, and with him gone and her dad being the abuser he was, the future didn't look too bright. She had to take care of herself. 'It was clear no one else was going to,' she thought to herself and wondered why people had kids if they didn't want to take care of them. The thought of being unwanted almost made her cry but she had to stay strong and keep a brave face for Jay. She couldn't let him know how lost she felt.

She took a deep breath and looked up across the street. In front of them was a huge cemetery, with acres of graves and mausoleums and a huge caretaker's house. She hadn't been inside for a long time, and her memory of it was vague. The place was surrounded by a huge iron fence with black metal bars that were charged with electricity. The only way in and out was through a main gate and it was monitored by a guard. 'The local gangs couldn't get in,' she thought to herself. 'It's the cemetery or nothing'.

Oddly, Jen wasn't scared of the cemetery. It just seemed peaceful and quiet. In her mind she almost felt drawn to it. She wondered what it would be like to hide out there. She would only be there when her parents fought. Trouble was, that was most of time when they were home. She studied the fence line and all the way down the street, until she saw it, a little wooden gate. It was probably locked, but there was enough room for her to slide in under it. She was thin and never had a problem squeezing into small spaces.

"Umm Jay...what about the cemetery?" Jen blurted out.

"Are you crazy? You can't get in there and even if you could, why would you want to? That place creeps me out."

"I think I can get in. There is a gate, and it has a small opening underneath and I think I could fit through."

"Someone would see you."

"Who? Nobody lives near the gate. It's near the abandoned houses. And I am sure no one lives in the house inside the cemetery. It's probably a caretaker's house that no one uses anymore."

"You can't be sure of that," Jay looked at her as if she was crazy.

"I think this will work and no one will see me at night. No one lives over there and if I slip in quickly enough, I will be fine."

Jay just looked at her in disbelief, "Do you really think you can pull this off?"

"Jay...I can do this. I have to do this. You can't just not go to school after all you went through to get in, and I don't see any other choice," Jen pleaded with him.

"Ok, you've convinced me. It's gotta be safer in there than out here at home."

"Now we just have to test my theory."

They waited until dark, and then Jen went about proving her point. She easily slipped through the gate and was inside with no one the wiser. Jay felt calmer, and at the same time creeped out. He had just agreed to leave his fifteen-year-old sister alone with his violent parents and her only outlet was a cemetery full of dead people. 'What could go wrong?" He thought sarcastically to himself. Jen looked around and decided that there was plenty of cover inside for her to hide from anyone who was looking for her. She just wasn't sure what to do if she had to spend the night.

As she turned to leave, she heard a sound. As quiet as a whisper, it sounded a lot like someone saying "Hello". She turned quickly thinking she had been caught. Fear rushed over her and she felt her face turning red. But as she spun around on her heels, she saw no one. There was only Jay guarding the gate she had come through. Jen convinced herself it was nerves and she had invented the whole thing in her head. She headed back to the gate and let herself out as easily as she came in.

As they walked away from the cemetery, Jen looked up to see a couple of the guys from the local gang heading in their direction. She grabbed Jay by the arm and drug him towards their yard. As the guys passed, they gave Jay a look. They knew he had gotten into a school and would be out of their reach soon. They weren't really happy about losing out on a new dealer.

"So, what do you do if you have to stay all night?" Jay asked.

"I don't know, I could go to the old house but only after I watch for a while to see that no one lives there. Maybe I will just go into one of the mausoleums if they are open." She laughed at the thought.

"If the weather was bad, that is not the worst idea. They probably do not lock them." Jay said shaking as if the idea scared him.

"Oh Jay, you're such a girl. Just picture the idea of sleeping in a room with dead people."

"Well, they are in coffins inside the walls you know. It's not like you will be propped up with your feet on one doing your homework." He laughed.

"Yeah, you've got a point. And it beats getting a broken arm or worse at home."

She remembered when Jay had gotten in the way one time when her dad had thrown a chair at their mother. It ended in a trip to the emergency room and a huge doctor bill that led to another fight when they got home. She didn't like the idea of ending up the same way. She didn't want to admit it to Jay, but she was a little scared. But if she had to do it, she would. She couldn't get in the way of his future.

"I feel a little better about the situation but I will still worry about you. Be careful of mom and dad, and watch out for the gangs. And please don't ever let anyone know you are in the house alone. Promise me!"

"I promise, I'll be careful and I will write to you as much as possible."

As Jen turned back to look at the cemetery, she felt a weird feeling overtake her. Almost as if she was being welcomed there. She studied the fence line, while sitting on the porch with Jay. As she looked at the gate, she was sure there was someone inside looking back at her. He was a blond-haired boy about her age she thought. She blinked in disbelief and when she focused again he was gone. She shook her head, and decided she had to be mistaken. No one could be gone that quickly. It all had to be in her imagination.

"Just promise me you will be OK," Jay said smiling at her.

She turned to him and made a goofy face, "You know I was always the smartest of us all."

"Yeah, I guess you are right, but I'm still your older brother and it's my prerogative to worry."

"Well don't! What's the worst that could happen? I could run into a ghost or something?"

They both laughed not wanting to let on to the other how scared they really were.

Chapter 1 The Escape

It didn't take a day's time before the fighting started up again. Jen's parents were louder than she had ever heard them and just as violent. She just couldn't understand how they could fight so much and stay together. She did know, she had to get out. Trouble was, getting out meant going through the room that had been designated ground zero. But even if she did get out, where would she go, it was 11 P.M.? It wasn't like she could just go to the library or a friend's house.

She quietly crept from her room and down the hall towards the living room. Ever so quietly, she tried to move without being heard or even worse seen. She peeked into the doorway just as a picture frame came crashing into the opening. Jen jerked back in fear. That was too close. She was able to jump past the opening of the doorway while her parents had their backs to her. In a few seconds, she was in the kitchen with her hand on the back-door knob.

Jen turned the knob and pulled the door gently towards her. She quietly prayed to herself that the hinges would not squeak. As soon as she had the door open just enough for her to slip through, she was out the door. She made her way into the yard before falling to her knees. The exhilaration and fear had her heart pounding in her chest. She knew, fear or not, she had to keep her head together and get to safety.

Jen didn't understand why her parents had to fight. She had been over it again and again in her head and it just didn't make sense. Her older sister Carrie said it was because they were just unhappy people. That didn't make sense to Jen. Just because you are unhappy, doesn't give you a reason to hurt other people and not act like a parent. None of her other friends had this problem, and sometimes, she wished she lived in one of their houses and could have a normal life.

She remembered the times when all the kids were still at home. When there were five of them, it was easier to stick together. But after her older brother Tim went to a correctional facility for getting mixed up with drugs and the local gang, and Carrie got a job away from the area, then there were only herself, Jay and little Johnny.

She tried not to think about Johnny. His was probably the cruelest fate of them all. She remembered the night when their parents started to break furniture and all the kids hid in the dining room. Johnny was too young to understand the fighting. He tore loose of Carrie's arms and ran from the house and into the road. Unfortunately, the car he ran in front of just couldn't stop in time. Jen thought that this might have been the point where her parents stopped caring about the kids all together.

The past year without the others was ok because Jen and Jay could hide easily together. But now Jay had gone to school and she was alone. For the first time there was no one there to protect her, and she knew what might happen.

She had no choice. If she was going to survive, it wasn't going to be at home. She had to go into the cemetery. When she and Jay went there originally, it didn't seem like such a bad idea. But now, facing the darkness of the place from the sidewalk just in front, she wasn't so sure. Her fears were overtaking her and she felt her hands start to shake. Could she really pull this off? She had to control her fear. There was no other choice. She had to do this one alone.

As she walked, Jen thought about how things were lately at home. Her dad had been away a lot with work and that seemed to make her mother happy. He worked construction and would be gone for a week at a time. Trouble was, he would come home and usually he would be tired and mean. Maybe work wasn't the only reason he stayed away. Maybe he just didn't want to come home or he had another place to go. Whatever he was doing, the family did not know for sure.

When he was home, he stayed to himself as much as possible. The kids didn't really approach him for fear of his temper. Everyone knew that when he was angry, it was better to be invisible. Jen's mother tried to be invisible at first but it didn't last for long. Especially if she had to ask him for money to pay the bills. A lot of their fights started with money and dealing with being a family.

Jen's mom worked as much as she could, and made a bit of money as a waitress in a bar, but it wasn't enough to pay the bills. That was what the latest fight was about, her mom in the bar around other men. Her dad wanted the money to come in but not if it meant his wife was around men.

Funny thing was, as much as Jen's dad wanted her mom to work and make money, he also wanted her home to do all the cleaning and do things around the house. No matter what they were doing, Jen felt invisible to them. She was sure of one thing; they weren't paying much attention to her. She barely remembered the last time her father spoke to her. It was a similar situation with her mother as well.

So, this is what it had all come to…standing on a street corner outside of a cemetery. Jen felt a chill shoot down her spine. The feeling was odd; she was feeling part fear, part exhilaration. She hadn't felt anything like it before, but at the same time she was excited. This felt like an adventure. It was a chance to get away from her life and craziness for just a little while. It was an escape.

She walked quickly to the little gate and paid close attention to her surroundings. If she was seen, this would be a one-time trip. Luckily, it was late at night and the tree lined streets were very dark. She scanned down the sidewalk and looked for anyone that might be able to see her. There was no one. As soon as she was sure it was safe, she slipped under the gate and was inside the cemetery wall.

In a few seconds, she found a hiding place inside a hedge of bushes. The growth was so thick, she was sure no one would see her. Her heart was racing in her chest and she could feel it thumping. She did it! She was proud of herself. She thought to herself, 'If she had to hide in a cemetery, this wasn't so bad.' Jen leaned back against a tree, folded her arms around her knees and took a deep breath and sighed in relief. She quietly giggled to herself and was so proud of what she had accomplished.

She had never thought about what it would be like to be inside a cemetery at night. The closest she got was that day before Jay left. It wasn't nearly as bad as she would have imagined. What was there to be afraid of? Everyone was dead. She was warm enough sitting in her pile of leaves in the hedge. The fall weather had not turned too cold.

As she calmed herself, and her heart rate went back to normal, she scanned the cemetery. Had anyone lived in the old house on the grounds? Jay said it was a caretaker's house but did anyone use it anymore? She decided not. If someone lived there, then there would be lights on or people moving around. These were things she never saw when she looked at the house. She stared at the house and studied its features as much as she could in the dark. It looked abandoned and lonely. Kind of like her.

As she looked at the house, she realized it had no curtains downstairs. If someone lived there, the windows would be covered in blinds or something. The house had older features like the ones from old pictures. The front porch had detailed carvings around the top of the roof. They were pretty but people didn't do that anymore. And the walls were covered in paint that was peeling after years of exposure. She decided it was a house like her grandma would have once lived in.

For a moment, Jen thought about a happier time when her grandma was still alive. Things were different then, she hadn't realized it until now. Her grandma's house was nice and filled with nice things. The more she thought about it, the bigger the lump in her throat became. She never really spoke of grandma and didn't really think about her that much.

A flood of memories came back, about her childhood and how the family lived with grandma that time her dad had left for a long time. Her mom had to work a lot to pay the bills and was not around much. Grandma took care of them all. It wasn't easy on her since she was ill a lot, but she loved the kids so much. She would tell them stories and make them her special cookies. Jen thought there was nothing better than grandma's cookies and one of her stories. She wouldn't have minded some of those cookies and a story now. She was getting hungry and the comfort of a story would have done wonders for her. A fantasy story had to be better than where was now.

Thinking of grandma brought a smile to her face, but it also made her think about her brothers and sister. Where were they and what were they doing? She laughed to herself, when she felt sure they weren't hiding in a cemetery in the middle of the night. A shiver ran down her spine again. She was kind of cold when the wind blew, but the feeling was almost as if she was being watched. The thought made her more than a bit paranoid.

Jen glanced around and saw no one, but she still felt the feeling as if someone was there. She became restless and thought that she might need to explore a bit to see what might be a round. She knew it would not be a good idea to go home until morning. The lights were still on at her house and she could see her mom and dad still moving around. Besides, she didn't want to creep back in, just to wind up in the middle of their fight.

Jen decided she needed a place out of the direct path the wind. The temperature wasn't that bad, but the grass under the leaves was a bit damp. She didn't want to chance the house. Even if no one lived there, there might be a watchman who checked the grounds at night. Perhaps the mausoleum, which was just a few yards away. If she made a break for it, the hedges would protect her from being seen.

As she tried to work up the nerve to move, there was a weird noise in the distance. Jen couldn't quite make it out but it sounded mechanical. As she focused on the sound, it got closer and closer. The sound was like a mechanical engine. She tried to determine what direction it was coming from. As the sound got louder, she looked around the cemetery road ways and saw a light headed right for her. She thought to herself that maybe hiding in a cemetery was not a good idea after all.

The sound was louder now and the light shined in her direction. Her heart sank in her chest, she was sure she was caught, by whoever or whatever it was.

Mass Destruction

Chapter 2 At Night in The Cemetery

Jen didn't know what to do. If she ran, she would be seen and if she stayed, she most certainly would be found. She decided the best thing to do was stay curled up behind the bushes and see what happened. The noise was right behind her and the light lit up the whole area where she was hiding. She looked through the bushes and saw what was coming, and to her amazement, her fear faded immediately. It was a short fat man on a motor scooter. She almost laughed at how comical the man looked. In her mind he kind of looked like a circus clown. At once she realized he was not coming for her, but making rounds on the road behind her.

The little scooter turned the corner beside her and moved away. As soon as he was out of sight, she laughed. How could she have panicked so much over a fat guy on a scooter? And then she thought, maybe this was what she needed, to convince herself that she was safe.   Her fear was gone now and a weird sense of calm filled her. But what was she to do now?

She was sure there would not be any more security runs for a while. Why would they need to continuously check the grounds? But if she was going to be coming here often, she would have to figure out the guard's schedule. But for now, it was almost 1 A.M., and it was getting colder. She decided that shelter was necessary, and the house might be too dangerous. Even though the guard did not check the house, it still seemed too risky. Her only other option was the big mausoleum.

Jen jumped to her feet and worked her way around the hedges as fast as possible making her way to the door. As she reached out for it, her heart began to beat loudly again. She quietly chanted to herself, "Please be unlocked, please be unlocked, please be unlocked." And to her surprise, it was, she moved inside quickly, hoping she wasn't seen by anyone.

As she made her way in, the inside of the room was very dark. Her eyes were used to the darkness outside, but it was even darker in the mausoleum. She closed the door behind her and stepped in as far as she dared without knowing where she was going. Within a minute or two, her eyes adjusted to the room. There were only two windows and both of them were covered with multicolored stained glass. The light coming through them was very little and did not illuminate the room well enough to see.

She moved towards the bigger of the windows and could see the shapes in the glass with the help of a local street light. It was a beautiful scene that looked like something from the bible. Since her family wasn't very religious, she couldn't place the image, but it looked like something her grandmother had shown her as a child when she would read stories to the children. The familiarity was comforting for a moment. The rest of the place however, was not so much. She could now see the place more clearly. Everything looked like stone or marble and it all reminded her of a cold smelly basement.

She moved from wall to wall trying to make out as much as she could. The place seemed to be clean. But then again, why would it be dirty? It's not like people would be coming and going through there like a normal house. Jen giggled and said to herself, "It's actually cleaner than home." She thought this must be true because her mother didn't really try to keep the place up and had often put the housecleaning off on the kids. But as they got older and left one by one, the amount of maid's service was pretty much all gone. All that was left was Jen now, and with school and the fights, it was near impossible for her to do much.

Jen walked around close to the walls and ran her fingers over the small squares that were in several places. Each had been engraved with about a sentence or two on it. It was hard to read, but what she could not make out with her eyes, she could sometimes feel with her finger tips. It seemed a lot of these people interned here were from decades ago and a few from as much as a hundred years before. She found it fascinating that people from a single family had continued to bring their relatives here. Jen thought long and hard about how close this family must have been, and how she barely remembered where her grandmother was buried. She hadn't visited her once over all these years. She decided if she could see her way through all this, that would be one thing she would correct.

While walking around Jen's eyes had adjusted as well as they could to the low light and she found the place to be more inviting than earlier. After all, she thought, who in the mausoleum was going to object to her being here or bother her. She had seen a bench on one wall. She had earlier kicked it accidentally and she decided this was as good a place as any to relax and settle in for the night.

As she leaned back, she felt something odd behind her head. It felt like something sticking out of the wall. She ran her hand over it and realized that one of the marker stones had a picture attached to it. She ran her fingers across it to try and clear the little dust that had collected. She could barely make out the image in the dark, bit appeared to be a very good-looking boy, probably a teenager, but she was not sure. His name however she was sure of ... Daniel. He had died in the 1960's. How sad she thought, that he could have died so young. She thought of her brother and how many other people were here in the cemetery that barely lived before they were gone. The thought made her sad.

She wondered what Daniel's life might have been like. She had always loved TV and movies and thought he might have been like James Dean or something back in the time when guys wore leather jackets and drove classic cars. She liked this version of him and decided she would hold on to it. It was comforting to think about Daniel. He was taking her mind off of everything else. It didn't do much for the chill in the air though. It was nice to be inside, but all the stone was adding to the coldness of the place. She was just happy to be dry and out of the wind though.

Jen decided if she was to come back here again, then next time she would bring a backpack with a few things. A flash light was a must, and something to eat and some water. She would need a sweater or something to wrap up in. She wished she had all these things right now, but there was nothing she could do about it. She just curled up into a ball on the bench and laid her head back onto Daniel's stone. Jen had never thought about the idea of having a boyfriend, but Daniel, she thought, might be a lot like what she would have wanted. Well, if he was alive and in her time. Sad thing was…he wasn't.

Jen's eyes grew heavy and she steadily drifted off to sleep. She knew she was in for the night and creeping back home would be a mistake. Besides what if the fight was still going on? She put the whole thing out of her head, yawned and was out. As she dreamed, her mind was filled with images of Daniel. She didn't even know him and she dreamed of him like she had known him her whole life. Her life was different in the dreams, there was no fighting, she was safe and he was there to protect her. The dream made her happy. She felt like she needed protecting, now more than ever.

At around 3 A.M., she jerked awake. She heard a noise but didn't quite know what it was. She was very groggy and out of it. It took a few minutes to focus. The sound happened once, then again. She thought to herself, 'Could it have been the security guard again?' Had she slept through one of his rounds? She wasn't sure. Then it happened again, it was a funny sound, but not the scooter. It almost sounded as if it was in the room with her. She panicked and thought to herself, 'Oh no, is someone here with me?'

She sat up and scanned the room but saw no movement. It didn't make sense, but the sounds were coming every few minutes and were getting a little louder. She stood up and walked around the room trying to make sense of what was going on. As she moved about, the sound got quieter like she had moved further away from it. The noise was really only loud when she was near Daniel. She thought maybe that is why it was loud enough to wake her from her sleep. Jen had rested her head near the source of the noise. It wasn't really loud at all, just coming from the wall.

Jen whispered out loud, "Hello". It was almost as if she was expecting a response. But none came. Just the occasional popping noise. The noise sounded electrical, but why would a cemetery put electricity into a place like this? It wouldn't make sense. "The dead have no need for lights," she thought to herself. And just as soon as she finished her sentence, the popping noise happened several times in a row.

The sound didn't scare Jen as much as it puzzled her. She wanted to know what it was and if she was safe, but at the same time she did not feel like she was in danger. She sat back down and turned to Daniel and said, "If you were here, you would protect me. Wouldn't you?" She knew it was silly to speak to him as if here were there, but since there was no one to answer her, she didn't care. Just as soon as she was done with her question, a series of pops happened again. Almost as if it were an answer to what she said.

Jen didn't know what to make of it all. She did realize how tired she was and she really needed more sleep. She curled back up like before and drifted off to sleep again. As she slept, her hands were tucked under her head and in between herself and the stone with Daniel's name on it. Her last thought as she was fading out, was how much she wished she could talk to Daniel. And then she was asleep again.

During the night she slept through the rounds the guard made and even the popping noises that were now even louder than before. The sounds had begun to take a new form now, almost like a version of Morse Code. It was probably just as well that Jen could not hear them, or know that she was not alone anymore.

Mass Destruction

Daniel walked
in the land of
the dead.
Now the dead
want him
back!

For Information About

From The Dead
Of Night
The Book Series Visit
gwmullins.wixsite.com/books

About the Author

Thanks for choosing this book, if you enjoyed it, please leave positive feedback.

G.W. Mullins is an Author, Photographer, and Entrepreneur of Native American / Cherokee descent. He has been a published author for over 12 years. His writing has focused on the paranormal and Native American studies. Mullins has released several books on the history/stories/fables of the Native American Indians.

Among his books are the extremely successful *Star People, Sky Gods, And Other Tales Of The Native American Indians*, *The Native American Story Book - Stories Of The American Indians For Children Volumes 1-5*, *The Native American Cookbook*, and *Walking With Spirits Native American Myths, Legends, And Folklore Volumes 1 Thru 6*.

He has released the complete series from his Sci/fi Fantasy Series *From The Dead Of Night*, including the Best-Selling titles - *Daniel Is Waiting*, and *Daniel Returns*.

His most recent work includes the new series ***Rise Of The Snow Queen*** featuring ***Book One The Polar Bear King***, ***Book Two The War Of The Witches*** and ***Book Three The Story Of Gerda And Kai.*** He has also released ***Messages from The Other Side*** a nonfiction book about communication with the dead.

For further information, on his writing, visit G.W. Mullins' web site at ***http://gwmullins.wix.com/books***.

<u>Also Available From G.W. Mullins</u>

Rise Of The Snow Queen Book Three The Story Of Gerda And Kai

Rise Of The Snow Queen Book Two The War Of The Witches

Daniel Awakens A Ghost Story Begins– From The Dead Of Night Prequel

Daniel Is Waiting A Ghost Story – From The Dead Of Night Book One

Daniel Returns A Ghost Story - From The Dead Of Night Book Two

Daniel's Fate A Ghost Story Ends - From The Dead Of Night Book Four

Rise Of The Snow Queen Book One The Polar Bear King

Dream Walker Book One Enter The Sand Man

Nick Grainger Book One The Curse Of Cleopatra

Dream Walker Book Two Wide Awake In Dream Land

The Legend Of White Bear

Messages From The Other Side Stories of the Dead, Their Communication, and Unfinished Business

Vengeance

Mysteries Of The Unseen World – Ghost, Hauntings and The Unexplained

Haunted America Stories Of Ghost, Hauntings And The Unexplained

Timeless – A Paranormal Romance Murder Mystery

Star People, Sky Gods, And Other Tales Of The Native American Indians

More Star People, Sky Gods, And Other Paranormal Tales Of The Native American Indians

Lost Tales Of The Native American Indians Vol 1

Walking With Spirits Native American Myths, Legends, And Folklore Volumes One Thru Six

The Native American Cookbook

Native American Cooking - An Indian Cookbook With Legends And Folklore

The Native American Story Book - Stories Of The American Indians For Children Volumes One Thru Five

The Best Native American Stories For Children

Cherokee A Collection of American Indian Legends, Stories And Fables

Creation Myths - Tales Of The Native American Indians

Strange Tales Of The Native American Indians

Spirit Quest - Stories Of The Native American Indians

Animal Tales Of The Native American Indians

Medicine Man - Shamanism, Natural Healing, Remedies And Stories Of The Native American Indians

Native American Legends: Stories Of The Hopi Indians Volumes One and Two

Totem Animals Of The Native Americans

The Best Native American Myths, Legends And Folklore Volumes One Thru Three

Ghosts, Spirits And The Afterlife In Native American Indian Mythology And Folklore

War Song: Tales Of The Native American Indians

Origin Tales Of The Native American